I took a deep breath, my eyes panning over the grandeur of the lake one last time, before turning the key in the ignition. I didn't want to leave, but the road awaited. Nothing happened when I turned the key. I grimaced, frustrated by Dorothy's sudden rebellion. Soon, she'd be the only family I had left in the world and she was trying to jump ship, too. When I noticed that the headlight knob was turned all the way to bright, I let my head crash down on to the rim of the steering wheel. I cried for far longer than a man can safely admit.

PRAISE FOR THE WORKS OF JOSHUA BADER

"Debut author Bader introduces readers to the Modern Knights series with an extremely impressive first novel of delicious urban fantasy with just a hint of romance. This fantastical thrill ride is filled with perfectly timed pop-culture references, stunning plot twists, and the snarky (and sometimes offensive) stylings of Colin's inner voice. Well-researched and creatively presented humor and action perfectly blend with moral quandaries in this outstanding debut."

- Publishers Weekly Starred Review

"I LOVED THIS BOOK. Did you see those caps? Yes, I'm that excited about it! Bader has written a great addition to the urban fantasy genre. His writing style has resulted in relatable characters who aren't all powerful (just like you and me). The resulting novel takes the reader on a wild ride from start to finish as you learn about Colin Fisher and his powers. Great stuff and can't wait for the second book!"

- GoodReads Reviewer, Cora Burke

"I must say upfront, this book exceeded my expectations! It was a thrill from beginning to end. Excellent writing, a wonderful plot, and a wonderful cast of characters kept me up longer at night than I wanted to see what was going to happen to Colin. Very highly recommend."

- Librarian, Penny Noble

FROSTBITE

MODERN KNIGHTS

BOOK ONE

JOSHUA BADER

CITY OWL
PRESS

FROSTBITE
Modern Knights: Book One

CITY OWL PRESS
www.cityowlpress.com

Cover design by Tina Moss. All stock photos licensed appropriately. Edited by Yelena Casale.

For information on subsidiary rights, please contact the publisher at info@cityowlpress.com.

Print Edition ISBN: 978-0-9862516-9-6

Digital Edition ISBN: 978-1-5242152-1-7

Printed in the United States of America

To my Dad

Who nightly introduced me to urban fantasy

Through magic rings that sent and brought back,

A horse that could talk,

And a wardrobe that sometimes led between Here and There.

- Joshua

PART ONE

CONVERSATIONS WITH THE DEAD

"The real problem with talking to the dead isn't getting them to

speak. It's getting them to shut up again once they start.

-Jadim Cartarssi, Armchair Necro-psychologist

1

With a name like Fisher, it's only natural for me to be attracted to large bodies of water. I'm easily impressed by anything deeper than a bathtub. I grew up in Denver until I was 14. It's a great city, especially for nature lovers, what with the ever-present mountains and an environmentally conscious population. Water, however, wild, free-standing, blue-as-the-sky, shiny-as-a-mirror, water was not Denver's strong suit. The "lake" within walking distance of my childhood home would barely merit mention as a puddle in other places of the world. Fortunately, in the ten years since my dad sent me packing, I've gotten to see plenty of those other places: West Coast, East Coat, Gulf Coast, Great Lakes.

In the era of quick status updates, where everyone can define themselves by a short list of labels and in 140 characters, my status depends greatly on the perspective of the person describing me (and their degree of relatedness to me). I've never used Face-space or Five-corners, so I'm at the mercy of the people who do when it comes to labeling. The ones that have floated back to me are "world traveler," "professional vagabond," "dabbling wizard," or "lunatic-just-short-of-civil-commitment." My dad once used the phrase "career criminal" when he thought I was out of ear shot. Those labels all fall short of the one I prefer: Colin Fisher.

The lake stretched out in front of me was a prime example of everything that pond in Colorado wasn't. Lake Thunderbird was man-made, but that didn't make it any less impressive to the eye. The way the wings of the lake wrapped back around me created the illusion that I was on the edge of an island beach, rather than a hundred yards from a State Park parking lot. Sitting against the thick oak trunk, staring out across the charcoal blue waters, I felt a million miles away from all my problems. That thought, unfortunately, reminded me that I was really only 682 miles away from my most pressing issue. It would be a nine-hour drive, if I pushed straight through.

Going home to Colorado was the last thing I wanted to do. My mom died when I was 14. Dad and I did not deal with her death too well. When we weren't crying, we were fighting. Most of the time, we fought because one of us had caught the other one crying: machismo at its dysfunctional peak. Adolescent males are crazy to start with, but the grief made me a royal pain in the ass. In my defense, my father could have been a little more supportive, more understanding. There's no use rehashing that argument now, I suppose. There's not enough time left to finish it.

When school let out that summer, my dad sent me to live with my aunt and uncle in Boston. The plan was I'd come back in the fall, once things settled down, got back to normal. I don't think my dad or I ever realized that without Mom, there was no normal. If we had tried, maybe we could have come up with a new normal, but we didn't. The last time I saw him in the flesh was at my high school graduation...in Boston, not Denver. I celebrated my twenty-fourth birthday three months ago, which

made me a Cancer. My dad had cancer and was either dying or
already dead.

My thoughts wandered like the wind-chopped waves on the
lake, dancing through graveyards of memories better left buried
and undisturbed. The book I brought out there with me was lying
in the brush beside me, untouched. Most museum curators
would kill me for carrying it around, let alone setting it down in
the dirt, leaves, and dried mud. I'll have to add them to the long
list of people who sternly disapprove of my behavior. I picked up
this peculiar tome in Charleston, chomping at the bit to read it.
It's not every day that I found a 17th century commentary on
faeries of the Rhine plains for less than ten bucks. The owner of
the antique store couldn't read Yiddish and thought of it as a cute
decorative paperweight. I thought of it as a feast of knowledge,
waiting to be devoured, and I suppose both of us were right, in
our own way. I probably would've finished studying it already, if
I hadn't called home to Boston that night.

I went to Harvard for three years. That was part of the initial
allure of spending the summer with Uncle James and Aunt Celia
in Massachusetts. By getting a feel for the area while I was still in
high school, my dad thought it might reduce the stress of
transition later. He always thought I had Ivy League potential. I
guess it worked a little. My freshman and sophomore years were
great. Then Sarai disappeared. I dropped out after the second
semester of my junior year, a ripe old burnout at the age of 20.
I've often wondered if my dad would have put a "My son is a
Harvard dropout" bumper sticker on his car if I sent him one. As
failures go, it's impressive: aim for the stars; when you crash,
you'll make a bigger crater.

I reached for the book, anxious to face the road again and be
done with it. My legs were stiff, but responsive, as I rose. In my
wild gypsy days, I've mastered the art of sitting under a tree for
long periods of time, without letting body parts fall asleep. The

walk from the lakeside to my car, Dorothy, was all too short. Dorothy's hood stretched on forever, a giant silver space-age yacht cleverly disguised as an '86 Ford Crown Victoria. Spare me the save-the-world speech: I had her converted to bio-diesel five years ago. It's possible to be environmentally responsible and still drive a tank.

I deposited the book onto the passenger seat, unceremoniously dumping it on top of the other unread treasures I'd acquired in the last week. My dad was lying in a hospital, parts of him slowly devouring other parts of him, but I still couldn't force myself to hurry. My traveling routine was what it was: drive for two to three hundred miles, refuel, cruise around the town to see if anything catches my interest, then find a safe place to park the car for the night. Interest for me comes in two forms: money and knowledge. I love old books and I don't mind a little manual labor to acquire them. I've been stretching my runs to 400 plus miles lately, near the edge of Dorothy's fuel limit, and skimping on the work, but this was still the way I operated. I'll get there when I get there. The fact that I didn't want to watch my Dad die had nothing to do with my refusal to break routine…okay, maybe a little. Maybe a lot.

I took a deep breath, my eyes panning over the grandeur of the lake one last time, before turning the key in the ignition. I didn't want to leave, but the road awaited. Nothing happened when I turned the key. I grimaced, frustrated by Dorothy's sudden rebellion. Soon, she'd be the only family I had left in the world and she was trying to jump ship, too. When I noticed that the headlight knob was turned all the way to bright, I let my head crash down on to the rim of the steering wheel. I cried for far longer than a man can safely admit.

2

I don't want to give anyone the wrong impression of me. I was burnt out, worn out, used up, and scared as hell, but I didn't usually spend my evenings crying over a dead battery. Life may be a mean thing to inflict on a person, but we all got hit with it. Most of the time, I kept it together better than that.

Once I got my frustration out of my system, I did the only thing I could do and started walking. Most people would have called for help on their cell-phone-computer-thingamajig. I didn't, because I didn't own one. Most companies gave me dirty looks when I tried to give Dorothy's license plate number as my home billing address. I could overcome that difficulty when I wanted or needed something badly enough, but an iLeash didn't hold a lot of attraction for me. They tended to do funny things when I held them.

Funny things…it's almost easier to admit I was weeping than to talk about such things. Tears, death, and the supernatural are not casual conversation topics. Let's just leave it at the fact that me and anything Internet-related just didn't get along. Most of the time, such devices flat-out refused to work for me. On the rare occasions that they did function, I usually ended up wishing they hadn't. It's a horrific curse, given how much I loved computers growing up. But Web abstinence is preferable to having another conversation with my deceased mother. Death can change a person.

The sun managed to flip below the horizon while I was still bemoaning my bad luck behind the wheel. The days were getting shorter, as October wound through its appointed course. It wasn't that cold tonight, but my whole body shuddered at the memory of my mom's voice.

"And that's not even the strangest of it …."

"Shut up, nobody asked for your opinion."

Everybody has a dark cobwebby voice that whispers to them from the hidden nooks and crannies of their mind. Mine was just a little bit louder and better developed than most.

"Right, I'm just part of your subconscious, not an invading alien intelligence from outside the fabric of space and time. Nothing to see here, move along."

"Hey, I know where the imaginary gag is at. Don't make me use it," I snarled back at it.

"Yessah, mastah. I be good. I be good."

"That's more like it."

Driving in, the entrance to the lake had been fifteen minutes from the interstate. I remembered passing a gas station and a bar about halfway from I-40 to the park, so my best guess was it'd be a half-hour on foot. I've been hiking in the growing darkness for about that long now, but there was no sign of civilization yet. It was only eight o'clock, but night was settling fast. Out East there's so much light pollution, I forgot what night really was. Walking along a country road in Oklahoma didn't offer the same illusion. Here, the primordial dark of night still lived.

Human low-light vision is mechanically different from our normal daytime sight. Color belongs to the sunlit lands and helps us spot ripe fruits from a distance with relative ease, distinguishing the red of the apple from the green of the leaves. In the dark, it's all shades of grey. The hours after sunset lend a film noire tint to the world. It made even a tame wood, one regularly disturbed by human presence, seem strange and savage to the senses. I knew that those woods had been culled free of major predators for decades, but that fact didn't register with my reptile brain. I refused to leave sight of the road.

I'd been rambling for over three years, but I could still get spooked. Rambling was my uncle's word for it, but it fit as well as anything. After Sarai, after Harvard, I couldn't stay in Boston. I packed up the stuff that mattered into Dorothy, sold the rest, and hit the road. I had a few thousand dollars saved up for a wedding and honeymoon that was never going to happen. I called home to Uncle James and Aunt Celia once a week, usually on Saturday nights. Aunt Celia, child of the sixties, thought I was looking for something. Uncle James thought I was nuts, but was far too polite to say it out loud. I couldn't blame him: we Fisher men have a history of losing our minds over women.

Tonight, I was out looking for something: a new car battery or a kind stranger willing to give me a jump start. My wallet would have preferred a good Samaritan, but it would survive an auto parts store. I had spent six weeks in August and September working at a Renaissance Fair outside Atlanta and made surprisingly good money at it. Apparently, my unkempt brown mane made me look like a young Merlin. I was scared I just resembled a young Charles Manson.

Up ahead, the black, white, and grey of the evening forest gave way to the electric red of a roadside sign. I was too far away to make out what it said, but the presence of color was comforting. Nothing was going bump in the night, no phantasmal chains were clanking, but I was not alone in the dark woods all the same.

"We're not alone, you mean. You're never alone," my internal voice piped in.

"Try not to remind me. Any ideas what it could be? It doesn't feel fairy-esque."

"Not a clue. But are you sure it's out in the woods?"

"What do you mean?"

"The light from the sign. A creepy scarlet like that…on a moonless night. I bet it paints everything under it in shades of blood."

"Quit it. The moon's in the first quarter tonight. Besides, light means electricity and electricity means people."

"Light usually does mean people. That's why bugs are drawn to it. It's where the food is at."

I pushed him down, mentally shoving a cherry red ball gag into the hidden alcove of my upper right brain cavity. It silenced him, but I couldn't help dwelling on the thought. I was close enough to see that the billboard was for the gas station, now, but…If I had been a hungry nocturnal predator of the forest, I might have followed the red beacon in hopes of a two-legged meal.

3

U nder the fluorescent lighting of the convenience store, with honky-tonk music drifting in from across the street, it was hard to maintain such morbid fantasies. Jubilantly colored displays of celebrities and cartoon characters hawking sugary snacks dominated one corner. Like thousands of other such stores, there was a snack aisle, a hygiene-slash-travel product aisle, and an automotive repair aisle. The far wall past those three rows was given over to quietly humming refrigerated cases. I had been in this same store a million times before, but never at that exact location.

I hadn't realized how hungry I was until I walked down the candy aisle. Almost without thought, I grabbed a king size Snickers bar. I waved it over my head and called out to no one in particular, "Don't worry, I'm paying for this." I promptly tore into it before I had even reached the end of the shelves. Nothing like a good cry and a long hike to get the stomach growling.

Past the engine cleaners, I found a box that looked promising: a portable jump-start kit. I studied the back of the box to see if it needed to be charged ahead of time. The one in my hand claimed to work straight out of the box. The price tag made me wince, especially when I remembered that I'd still likely need to replace the battery in the next couple of days. Still, any port in a storm, and I was adrift in a virtual hurricane. I finished my candy bar and tucked the box under my arm.

Caffeine and sugar would help on the walk back, so I took a tour of the coolers. A Dr. Pepper called out to me behind frosted glass, but I jerked my hand back upon contact with the fridge handle. The chrome was frozen to the touch, so cold that I left a good sized skin sample. I stared at it curiously for a long moment before deciding that coffee might be better suited for an October night anyway. The pot looked suspicious and I was certain this same java had been sitting here, slowly charcoaling, when I drove past on my way down to the lake several hours prior. I dumped one, and then another, Irish cream packets into a Styrofoam cup before pouring the dark brew on top. The cream told me a lot about my mood. I always take my coffee black unless I'm scared or angry. I thought I was coming out of my funk, but my drinking habits suggested my subconscious was still deep in the mire.

"Mmph mmmrr pphhmmm."

"Stop struggling. I'm not letting you back out so you can mock me."

I grabbed a second Snickers and headed for the register. I didn't realize, until after I unloaded everything on to the counter, that no clerk was in attendance.

"Hello? I'm ready to check out."

The only answer was silence. The longer I waited, the more certain I became that the attendant was lying on the other side of the counter in a pool of his own blood. Had I missed an armed robbery by mere minutes? I shook off the paranoia and called out again.

"Mmmph Grrmmt."

Leaving my prizes by the register, I stepped back through the front door. There was a battered old truck parked off to one side. Across the street, six or seven cars were gathered around the bar. The muffled sound of Hank Junior coming out of it was a welcome relief to the cold quiet of the gas station. I glanced over the door, hoping to see a "Be Back Soon" or, in more regionally appropriate vernacular, "Getting a Beer, Hold Your Horses" note. No such sign was in evidence. I slipped back inside.

"Hello?"

I didn't want to peek behind the counter, but as the seconds of emptiness stretched into minutes, I saw no other choice. The gray and white linoleum tile was mercifully empty. No dying store clerk, no pools of blood, no signs of struggle or violence.

"Rrmmh Mmmph Mrmm."

So where was he? I knew this was the Bible Belt, where people were generally trusted to do the right thing. But I'd been in here for at least fifteen minutes and hadn't seen a soul. If I had a buddy and a moving van, I could have looted the entire store. I mentally added up my purchases, pulled three twenties from my wallet and weighted them down by the beef jerky jar next to the cash box. I thought about writing a note, when I noticed the door to the back room.

I slowly walked over to it, past the row of whispering coolers. The machines glared out at me with their mechanical blue light. The air was colder here, forcing goosebumps to the surface. When I knocked on the door, the wood underneath felt like ice. On instinct, I took a deep breath and pulled my aura in, picturing it as a thin white shell-skin stretched tight around me. It was the first spell I had ever learned, a defensive magic so familiar I could use it on reflex. As spells go, it was little more than a token gesture of protection, but I felt better afterwards anyway. My confidence restored, I knocked again, noticing the cold did not bother me as much.

"Hello? Anybody back there?"

When no response came, I tried the handle. The door swung in six inches before stopping against something hard. My breath came out as a solid white fog as the chilled air rushed back from the opening. What I did next should prove how spectacularly short-lived I would be in a horror movie: I squeezed my head through the opening to see what was blocking the door. Any Hollywood ax murderer worth his grinding stone would have pounced at that point.

There was no ax murderer in evidence...just the body of the attendant wedged in the corner between door and wall. His skin and clothing were covered in a hoary white frost, his blue lips pulled apart in a soundless, frozen scream. I'm not an expert in anatomy, but I think the gaping hole in his chest was right where his heart used to be.

4

I stood behind the counter, eyes locked on that treacherous store room door. I didn't need a mirror to know how pale my skin was. No doubt I looked like a zombie clerk extra from a Night of the Living Dead remake. I knew what I needed to do, but I couldn't quite force myself to start moving.

"Mmph...ptui. I tried to tell you it was too damn cold back there."

"What's the temperature mean? How did he freeze to death in the store's back room?"

"First, he didn't freeze to death. His heart was ripped from his chest AND he froze to death. From the looks of it, either one could have killed him. Second, store that formula away for later use: Cold equals bad, very bad. Right now, we've got more important things to worry about."

"Yeah, I know."

The smart money was on wiping down any surface I touched, taking the stuff I came for, and getting back to Dorothy ASAP. The cops rarely like occupations that can be summed up as aspiring vagrant. My alibi for the last day was less than stellar. I could imagine the interrogation now:

Cop: Mr. Fisher, where were you when he was killed?

Me: Sitting under a tree by the lake. Or maybe I was walking from my car to the murder scene.

Cop: Can anybody verify that?

Me: Well, there's a nice oak tree, but...do you have anyone on staff that speaks Plant?

The best I could hope for was an insanity plea. If I was lucky, whatever it was about me that fouled up smart phones and laptops had royally screwed up the store's surveillance system. If I hurried, I could be two states away before sunrise.

There's a lot of words that could be used to describe me: College dropout, weirdo loner, polyglot, wizard-wannabe. Unfortunately, lucky and amoral were not among them. The security system was working. Worse, I couldn't force myself to walk away from this. There was a chance I'd seen or heard something that might help the police catch the sicko who did this.

"If you pick up the phone to call 911, you'll regret it," my annoying inner voice warned.

"I don't have a choice. If I don't call the cops, it'll just make me look guilty."

"Colin, you really don't want to touch that phone."

I hesitated, but I lifted it from its cradle anyway. It was a land-line and as old as I was. No dial tone. I tried hitting 9 to see if that would let me call out. Still no dial tone, but the line wasn't dead silence either.

"Hello?"

There was no answer, but the background noise got louder. It sounded like heavy breathing...no, heavy panting, like a Saint Bernard after a long sprint. My eyes returned to the back door, still slightly ajar. I was suddenly wondering whether the man's heart was torn out or eaten out by a giant canine-esque maw.

"Whoever this is, you don't want to screw with me." I could only hope I didn't sound as scared as I was. "I know magic." I meant to say I had a gun, but the other slipped out before my brain-to-mouth editor could get a handle on it.

The panting stopped and for a moment the line was blessedly silent. A terrible voice spoke, a rumbling stone-edged tongue uttering words full of strange clicks and guttural stops. It growled its way through four or five alien sentences before falling back into silence. I slammed the phone back into its cradle.

"What the hell was that?"

"Cherokee, maybe. It was Native American, but I can't place it. And what are you asking me for? You're the linguistic genius."

"So you jump ship on the whole 'I'm just your shadow-side' thing when there's blame to be placed, but when I come up with all the good ideas ...."

"You know, I can find another gag."

"Okay, yeah. It was native. But it was OLD native."

"You're thinking Mayan or Incan?"

"Think older. Think whatever it was they all spoke before they came over the ice bridge."

"Did you catch any of it?"

"No, but I don't need to translate to know what it was saying. It was threatening to eat our heart out, too."

"That's about what I thought. Death threats have a rhythm all their own."

My internal monologue was shattered by the ringing phone.

BRRRINGG!

I stared at it, hand trembling.

BRRRINGG!

I reached, but I couldn't quite grab it before ....

BRRRINGG!

I snatched it up, determined to deal with the monster. "Look, I don't know who ...."

"Colin?" The speaker whispered, soft, distant, and breathless.

I was scared out of my mind, contemplating sorcerous counter-measures for an unknown assailant...but I still recognized that voice. "Dad?"

"Colin, Colin…I can't see you, Colin."

"Dad, it's all right, I'm here."

"Colin, I'm sorry. I'm sorry, I didn't tell you before…I know you didn't hurt that girl."

"Sarai. Her name was Sarai, Dad."

"Sarai." The sound was faint, as if the receiver were drifting away from his mouth. "I'm sorry I didn't handle it better. I knew…I knew you were a good boy, Colin. I'm sorry, sorry, sorrryyyy …."

I nodded, a single tear rolling down my cheek. "I'm sorry I didn't make it back soon enough. I would've liked to see you one last time. I love you, Dad."

I stood there with the phone pressed hard against my ear, hoping for an "I love you" that never came. The line, like my father, was dead.

FIRST INTERLUDE

T he gas station convenience store could have been a twin to the one outside Lake Thunderbird, Oklahoma: snacks, hygiene, dry goods, automotive accessories, and refrigerated items. At that other store, something very bad had recently happened. At this one, something very bad was in the process of happening.

Jacob Darien held the revolver casually, comfortably, but it was pointed at the clerk all the same. His tone of voice suggested this was old hat for him. "Two strips of beef jerky, five lottery tickets, and all your money. You want anything, Dizzy?"

The scantily clad redhead draped over his left shoulder picked up at the mention of her pet name. "Umm…bubblegum. Can I get some bubblegum, Jakey-poo?"

He looked at her and the clerk thought hard about the shotgun under the counter. "Really? My name in front of our guest?"

"You used mine first, my consort," Dizzy replied, only half chastised.

"I doubt they have a birth certificate on you." Jacob's tone softened, his accent changed. "Go forth and get thy gum, my child."

She kissed him on the cheek and went prancing off down the candy aisle. "Thank you, Reverend. Jakey was getting a little boring."

The clerk slowly lowered his hands to the register. "All right, all right, I don't want any trouble. You can have the money."

The robber's face had relaxed, gotten older, the voice more fatherly now. "Bless you, my son. It is the will of the goddess that you doeth thus. Do as thou are told and all will go well with you." He turned his head to the girl again. "My daughter, I shall require a Dr Pepper to quencheth my thirsteth."

He turned back just when the clerk had gathered the confidence to go for the gun. "I'm a doctor, too. My degree is in sophistry, young man. An excellent field of study for any man of the cloth, don't you think?"

The clerk shoved the money into a plastic sack, unable to think of how he should reply to that. "There you go."

The robber known as Jakey-poo and Reverend glanced down at the bag. "I believeth my host specifically requested beef jerky and lottery tickets as well. I do not bear false witness in this, do I?"

"Right, right," the clerk turned to the jerky jar. "I just…I've never been robbed before."

He put two sticks of dried meat on the counter, then reached underneath as if going for the scratch tickets. His right hand wrapped around the stock of the gun when the man spoke again. "Where is the rest of it?"

The man's voice had changed again. This time it held neither the casualness of the first nor the joviality of the second. Now he sounded like a cold-hearted British movie villain. The clerk's nerves froze at his tone.

Dizzy yelled from the coolers. "Hey, Mr. Osborne, you're not supposed to be out during a creative acquisition. Jakey-poo said so."

"He'll thank me later." The man's eyes never left the clerk. "This young man was just thinking about trying out his boss's gun."

The clerk whipped it out and leveled it at Jacob-Reverend-Osborne. "Maybe I am. Get the fuck out."

"Pull the trigger and you're a dead man," the robber growled.

"Ooo," Dizzy clapped, dropping three bottles of Dr. Pepper on the floor. "A real Wild West showdown." One of the bottles began spraying brown foam in every direction.

The voice returned to its initial bored coolness as he tilted his head down to his shoulder. "I've got this, Osborne." When he turned back to the clerk, there was no threat in his voice. "Put it down, Stephen. It's not your money, it's the store's. They'll never miss it. Insurance will repay them for every dime we take and then some. The only ones getting screwed over here are the insurance companies."

"I'm telling you man, get the fuck out, and take your freaky girlfriend with you. I don't want to call the cops, but I'm not ...."

He lost his voice when Jacob gestured with his free hand. The clerk had been so fixated on the gun hand, he barely noticed the motion. The shotgun leapt from his hands and sailed across the front toward the magazine rack. The robber never touched it, but it had been torn from his fingers all the same.

The last thing he remembered before he passed out was the girl, giggling with ecstasy. "Eek, we're showing off our magic. Yay, Jakey-poo...I mean, stranger I've never met before." As she jumped up and down, the clerk made note not only of her firm breasts, but also of the pair of fiery wings sprouting out of her back and the tiny curved horns appearing on her forehead.

Jacob hopped the counter, took five tickets off the Lucky 7's roll, then walked back around, stopping to pick up the shotgun.

He cracked it open like a pro. "No ammo." He tossed the gun toward Dizzy.

She caught it and moved up to kiss him. "Could come in handy anyway. Maybe goddess is telling us we need more firepower."

"More?" Jacob cocked an eyebrow at her. "Baby, you're already traveling with the three most powerful wizards on the planet and that's just what I'm packing in this body. What do you think we're here to do, start Armageddon?"

A dark voice answered Jacob from the depths of his subconscious.

"Pretty much. Shouldn't be too much longer before we can get the party started."

PART TWO

PROBLEM WITH AUTHORITY

"The mark of truth is that it's so obscenely complex when you get up close with it that it would drive you mad to stare at it for longer than ten seconds. Occam's razor isn't for understanding the world; it's for slitting your wrists and gouging out your eyes before such understanding turns you into a raving lunatic."

-Jadim Cartarssi, Amateur Philosopher and Part-time Raving Lunatic

1

hate to admit it, but that wasn't my first time in police
custody. I'd never been formally charged with anything more
serious than Public Nuisance, but I have been questioned on
everything from Jaywalking to Murder for Hire. It went with the
territory of using my car as my address of record. It wasn't
politically correct to say it out loud, but when something really
nasty happened, standard police procedure still involved rounding
up all the gypsies, tramps, and thieves.

Unfortunately, I wasn't just a shiftless vagrant. I was *the*
shiftless vagrant who found the body. One might think that
reporting a crime to the proper authorities would have granted
me a small measure of trust (and/or immunity from prosecution).
It hadn't. The only good news was that they hadn't officially
arrested me for anything yet. I think they were hoping I would be
decent enough to confess and save them the trouble of
investigating any further.

The first officer on the scene was off-duty at the time, a
county deputy who happened to be drinking at the bar across the
street. The alcohol made him friendly enough...until he saw the
body. From the retching sounds, I'm guessing that his liquid

courage was congealed in a puddle next to the deceased. After that, it was all sideways glances at me from a safe distance across the room.

Two uniforms from the nearest town arrived next. One of them took down my version of events, while the other spoke to the deputy, well out of earshot. I'm not sure what the townies made of it other than deciding that the whole incident was not a town matter. More calls were made and, within the hour, the gas station was host to a statewide law enforcement convention. I maintained my post by the counter the whole time, hoping the assembled criminalists might forget they had a convenient scapegoat on hand. Unfortunately for me, they remembered.

It was well after midnight before I was escorted to a holding cell. A holding cell is for "witnesses" who were going to be "questioned" and who were, in legal theory at least, not under arrest. I held no delusions about my freedom. If I tried to leave, they would arrest me for the murder just to keep me there, whether they really believed I did it or not. My best bet was to play along and hope either they figured out I didn't do it or I ran out the clock. Most states have rules regarding how long a suspect could be held without formal arrest, usually somewhere between 24 and 72 hours. I had no idea what the shot clock was in Oklahoma, but I was fairly certain there was one and it was slowly ticking in my favor.

They woke me up a little bit before five in the morning. I didn't even bother to ask about breakfast. Like I said, it's not my first time in police custody. True to form, they used the expected tricks: hard and fast while I was still waking up, a cold interrogation room, a wobbly chair, hunger, and a good cop/bad cop routine that was old when Abbot met Costello. The not-so-subtly implied message was that I could trade my confession for three meals a day and all the sleep I cared to get. Three different detectives took turns going over everything that happened at the store and my whereabouts, activities, attitudes, and habits over the last several months. I left out only the strange business with the phone call and personal information that I considered to be none of their business. Around noon, they gave up and sent me back to the holding cell.

I'm not proud to admit it, but when a guard brought me a plastic lunch tray, I ate its contents. I didn't have a clue what it was, but I forced it down. It was the color of refried beans, the texture of paste, and it smelled vaguely of sweat, shame, and mold. Man does not live by Snickers bar alone, though in a perfect world, he would be able to.

I lost track of time at that point. I dozed off and without window or clock, I was at a loss to know whether I'd slept fifteen minutes or fifteen hours, though it felt more like the former. My mind sloughed through recent events, processing it all for meaning. The human subconscious is an amazing tool and I trusted mine to eventually overlay order and purpose on my latest misadventures. I was no longer worried about making it to Denver quickly or what I would say to my father when I finally saw him again. My dad was dead and we'd already exchanged our parting apologies. It was better the way it happened. Face to face, we would have choked, unable to say those dreaded un-masculine words: I'm sorry. As I said earlier, though, death changes people.

2

I sat in a very different interrogation room compared to the Gulag predecessor they had me in this morning. This room was larger, cleaner, and more comfortable. There was no evidence of the base theatrics employed earlier. It might have made some people feel good, but the sudden switch made me nervous. If they didn't feel the need to hammer a confession out of me, they either had the killer (which was good) and needed me as a witness, *or* they had enough evidence to convict me if the case went to trial (which was very, very not good). The two video cameras in the room, both trained on my assigned seat, suggested the latter.

The door opened and a new detective came in. At least, I took her to be a detective, though she certainly didn't look the part. I guessed her to be five-four, with a pleasantly rounded shape that was easy on the eyes. Her straight brown hair provided an attractive frame for a face that appeared too young for such gruesome affairs as frozen men with missing hearts. She dressed like a detective, though: crisp, black pantsuit with a dark blue blouse. Her smile made a good effort at setting my heart aflutter, but my surroundings and recent experiences put a damper on the effect. There was something familiar about her, but I couldn't put my finger on it.

"Hi, I'm Special Agent Devereaux. I'm with the FBI." Her voice was soft and uncertain, almost making her statement sound like a question. She offered her hand and I shook it, despite my surprise. Her tone and body language were decidedly feminine, but her handshake and forearm spoke of restrained, solid muscle.

I smiled back, hoping it made me look more like Merlin and less like Manson. "Colin Fisher. I'm the wandering vagabond who stumbled onto the body."

She laughed a little. "It can't be any fun. Dying father, car trouble, and you end up in here. I'm not sure I could smile if I was in your shoes."

The longer I looked at her, the more certain I felt we had met before. I had been questioned by the FBI once before, but I think I would have remembered Agent Devereaux. "The freedom of the gypsy lifestyle has its own price tag. The car will get fixed sooner or later. You'll find the guy who did this. My dad ..." I let it trail off.

"Not many Harvard-educated gypsies out there." That made me gulp. I'd left out my educational background in the previous interviews with the locals. "I bet you've seen some pretty amazing things in your travels. Are you planning on writing a book about your experiences?"

I tried to keep my nerves out of my voice, but I didn't like the direction this conversation was headed. "No, I'm not much when it comes to travelogues. The joy is in being there, not reading about it. And I dropped out of Harvard, so I'm just a partially educated idiot."

"I know and I appreciate the honesty." She nodded, then leaned a little bit closer across the table. "I'm with the FBI's Behavioral Sciences Investigative Division. It's my job to know all about people."

I tried to think through the ramifications of that title and found it more than my brain could currently handle. My tongue started moving to put order to the chaos. "Behavioral Sciences means you're a profiler. Profiling means there is more than one body: a serial killer. And, right now, you're studying me, which means ...."

She shook her head, letting long auburn strands dance around her head. "Relax, Colin. I'm simply here to talk with you. We get called in for things like this sometimes. I have to talk to everyone."

"Okay."

"Not okay. This one is dangerous. You've got a stupid streak a mile wide for pretty girls."

"Colin, you told the detectives this morning that you drove here from Saint Louis and were on your way to Colorado because your dad was sick. Is that right?"

"Yes, ma'am."

"And your last stop before Lake Thunderbird was a travel plaza in Tulsa?"

"Yes, ma'am."

"Did you plan to stop at the lake?"

"No, ma'am. I had to backtrack off of I-44 to I-40 to find a natural gas filling station. I saw a sign on the Interstate for the lake and it sounded like a nice place to take a break. I'm a sucker for nature hikes."

She smiled again, her white teeth beaming a hypnotic signal a few shades too bright to be comfortable. Her eyes were a stormy blue and that somehow struck me as wrong. "I understand," she said. "My grandparents had a duck pond on their farm when I was a little girl. I loved spending time down by the water's edge." She paused as if lost in nostalgia, though I suspected her pacing was all part of some greater script. "What did you do while you were at the lake?"

"I walked around for a bit, let my legs stretch. The weather was nice, so I grabbed a spot under an oak tree and tried to read.

It didn't go too well. I couldn't concentrate...too busy thinking about my dad."

"I'm guessing you were not eager to get there. Family can be tough."

"She's fishing, Colin. Don't trust her."

I ignored my inner cynicism. If she wanted to play Dr. Freud with my childhood, I would let her. "Yeah, he's my dad, but we...we struggled after Mom died. When I dropped out of school, conversation went from strained to impossible."

I expected her to plunge ahead through the opening and ask me when my dad started molesting me, or whatever it was that psychologists cared about. She didn't, instead making an abrupt U-turn. "I saw the books in your car. Which one were you reading? Maybe I could get it in here to you...something to read between interviews."

I really didn't want to talk about my choice of literature. The only thing more suspicious than a vagabond was a vagabond obsessed with the occult. "Yiddish fairy tales from Germany." I forced myself to blush, as if I were an English professor caught red-handed with a Harry Potter novel.

"Yiddish? Are you Jewish, Colin?" She chuckled. "I'm sorry that came out wrong. I mean...it's an unusual language outside of certain subpopulations."

"No offense taken. Religiously, I'm Catholic. Race-wise, I don't know...Fisher is British, but my branch of the family is American Heinz 57. I just have a gift for languages."

"I'd say. What about this one? What languages are in it?" She slid a large folio-sized book on to the table, wrapped in a plastic evidence collection bag. It was as bad as I'd feared, I realized as I looked at the black leather cover shining under the fluorescent lights. I'd rather talk about my family dynamic than that damned book.

"Quite a few, I think. English, Aramaic, Sanskrit, Latin...might be a couple others."

"Careful, Colin."

"Damn it, you think I don't know that? This isn't going the way we want it to."

She asked another question, oblivious to the internal dialogue I had to drown out to hear her. "You don't know all the languages in the book?"

I shook my head. "A lot of side comments have been added helter-skelter by previous owners. It's a very old book."

"So you can't read it all?"

I bit my lips, not wanting to answer that question directly. Omitting the truth was one thing, but lying to the FBI didn't seem prudent if I could avoid it. Agent Devereaux of the straight brown hair, Irish white skin, and wrong-colored eyes waited for a moment before asking something else. "So what is it? I've never seen anything like it. Our analysts have a betting pool as to how much it's worth."

I tried to put a humble face on it. "I picked it up at an estate sale for fifty bucks."

"What do you think *Antiques Roadshow* would say it was worth?"

I shook my head. "I wouldn't be qualified to say," I allowed. "More than I paid for it."

She looked at it quizzically, as if afraid it might bite her hand if it came too close to its cover. "But what is it?"

"It's a hand-written copy of the Necronomicon. Supposedly it was made from Lovecraft's own notes rather than a printed edition."

"You don't want to talk about it, do you? You've gone pale." She patted my wrist gently. "It's okay. It's just a book, right?"

"Wrong."

"Yeah, it's just a book...but I'm not an idiot. In the heart of the Bible Belt, it's enough to get convicted for any number of things I didn't do."

"Okay." She pulled it off the table and tucked it away. "We

don't have to talk about it if you don't want to. What do you want to talk about?"

"I didn't do it. I'd like to talk about that. I was just in the wrong place at the wrong time. Why on Earth would I call the cops and stick around if I had anything to do with it?"

"Had you ever met the clerk before?"

"No. I drove by the place on my way to the lake."

She pulled out a notebook, flipped a few pages, then read four names off. "Do any of those names sound familiar?"

I shook my head. "No, but I've met a lot of people in my travels."

"Colin, I have to ask this, but have you done any drugs recently?"

Drugs? This was a new tack. "No, I mean, I've smoked weed before...used peyote, too, once. But that was years ago."

"She keeps jumping tracks. Maybe it's an interview trick, but it's almost schizophrenic. Like she's two people at once," my inner voice offered.

"If we took a urine sample right now, would it say any different?"

"No, I'm clean. You got a cup?"

"The deceased...Stephen Bausser...he had a rather large supply of crystal meth in his truck." She paused. "Are you sure no one asked you to wait around the store and get a package? It's not like you knew what would be in it, right?"

"She's soft-selling it, trying to give you a way to confess that doesn't make us look so bad. It's their theory: the kill was drug-related and we're the convenient doped out hippie from out of town."

"No, I've told you all a dozen times. I just needed a jump for my car."

She started to say something else, but as I looked at her, it all finally clicked into place and I interrupted her.

"That's why they sent you in here."

"Pardon me?"

"You look like her. Same height, hair color, build. It's why you spent so much time asking me warm questions you don't really care about. You're just getting me to talk to build rapport."

Agent Devereaux's expression changed, the soft, friendly femininity dissolving into trained steel. "Yes," she confessed, "You're far too intelligent for the amateur tactics they've been using."

"Flattery won't work, either. I can't take credit for a crime I didn't commit."

"What about Sarai?"

I closed my eyes and let the unspoken accusation slap me. Devereaux's resemblance to her was uncanny. The eyes should have been a deep forest hazel instead of a lake-water blue, a lone mistake. When I finally spoke again, my voice was quiet, but harsh, full of threat. "I didn't kill her, Agent Devereaux. I don't know where she went. She just disappeared."

"One evening she was there, in your apartment, by your own admission. In the morning, she was gone. Nobody's ever seen her since. Until ...." She let it hang.

I took the bait. "Until when?"

"We found the body, Mr. Fisher. Her heart was missing, too."

3

I leaned back in my chair. "Well, that's a relief. For a second, I thought you actually had some evidence."

That knocked the wind out of Agent Devereaux. "What?"

"You're lying. You know what I've learned on the road these last few years...it's how to read people. You're bluffing. You're working under the theory that I killed both people. Most serial killers have a signature, something unique to the way they kill. You guessed mine was cutting out the heart. Accordingly, you lied about finding her body, trying to make it believable by adding my supposed signature to it. You want to rattle me...you were doing a better job when you stuck to the facts."

"You're wrong, Mr. Fisher. Massachusetts State Police found her corpse two weeks ago."

"Agent Devereaux, I'm sure you are an amazing agent and that you're very good at your job. But your theory is flawed. I didn't kill the store clerk, which means I didn't remove his heart, which means it's not my signature."

"And Sarai? Are you admitting you killed her?"

"Not to you. Hell, I can't even get him to admit it to himself."

"Agent Devereaux, again, I'm sure you're a good investigator, but I'm well past my twenty-four hour holding period on that subject. If that's all you're going to ask me about, I assume I'm free to go."

She was about to answer when there was a knock at the door. When it opened, an older Hispanic man came in, his attire suggesting that he too lived on a federal salary. Agent Devereaux stood up, looking frustrated. "Sir, I can handle this."

He waved her off with his hand. She quickly left us, anger flashing in her stride. He gazed at me, curious, but waited till the door slammed shut before speaking. "I'm Supervisory Special Agent Rick Salazar." He didn't offer his hand.

"Colin Fisher, murder suspect," I snarked.

"Mr. Fisher, you're free to go. I'd like you to know that up front. Your lawyer is downstairs waiting for you. You don't have to say a thing to me without her present if you don't want to. But I'd like to talk to you, if you're willing."

"My lawyer?" I was genuinely confused. They hadn't offered a phone call, because I wasn't formally under arrest. I was shocked to hear I had a lawyer at all, much less one that was physically in the building.

"Can we talk? Off the record?"

I nodded. "Sure."

"First, you have my condolences. There's no easy way to say this, so I'll come right out with it. Your father passed away last night."

I almost said, "I know," but I didn't. Instead, I nodded again. "It's for the best. I heard he was in a lot of pain."

Agent Salazar sat down in the chair across from me. Our eyes met, but neither of us broke contact after the socially-sanctioned few seconds. His irises were a greyish blue flecked with purple and I felt a strange sense of safety and comfort in them. When he did break the gaze, he said, "I'm worried about you, Mr. Fisher.

I'm afraid we may meet again in a room like this. Do you know why?"

"I don't know what happened to Sarai."

"Yes, you do. Want me to tell you all about it?"

He shook his head. "Maybe you don't. But that's not why I'm worried. Isolation, Colin…it's the only symptom shared by every mental disorder. Without social connections, a support system, the mind can start playing tricks on you."

Internally, *You're telling me.* Externally, "I'll make it."

He continued, as if I hadn't spoken. "Factor in your intelligence, your choice of reading materials, and the losses you've endured…If you start losing your grip on reality and morality, you could be a very dangerous man. There are some profilers in the other room who think you already may be."

"Then why are you letting me go?"

"Because you didn't do this. Not the store clerk, not the others. But, Mr. Fisher," he held out a business card in his hand, "if you ever want help, call me. If you get in over your head and you want out, there are people who can help."

I tucked the card away in my jeans pocket. "I thought psychopathy was incurable."

He smiled, but it was a sad smile. "You're not a psychopath. You empathized with Agent Devereaux. It's how you got past her act; you sensed what she was really feeling instead of merely what she was showing. You're not a psychopath…but that doesn't mean you couldn't be a monster. Some of the worst predators are the ones who use their empathy to find the vulnerability in their victims." He locked eyes with me again. "Have you killed anyone yet, Mr. Fisher?"

"No."

"I believe you."

I looked away from his gaze. "Then why …?"

"… are we talking?" He thought about it for a minute, the

silence between us comfortable, not cop and suspect in interrogation. "I helped with the aftermath of the Columbine shootings early in my career. The more I learned about it, the more I wondered if the right person at the right time could have helped those boys do something different. I never met them. But I'm meeting you. If I can be that person, I want you to call me when the time is right."

"Look, I think I've got everything under control. But if I start to lose it ...."

"Start? We're well out of the starting gate of insanity, my friend."

"... I'll call you. I promise."

I stood up, ready to see this mysterious lawyer of mine and hunt down some dinner. "So how did they figure out I didn't kill that guy anyway?"

Agent Salazar looked grim. "There was another killing while you were in custody. Same MO." He shook his head. "Go bury your father, Mr. Fisher. Try and forget about this mess."

4

o fewer than three officers walked me downstairs to my
attorney. No doubt they were hoping I'd kill someone on
my way out so as to make my recapture simple. Their
manner was tight, closed-mouthed, and disciplined. Second body
or not, these men still believed me guilty of something. I
wondered how much the FBI had told the OSBI about Sarai's
disappearance.

I spotted her immediately, though lawyer was not the first,
second, or even third idea I connected to her. Her hair was an
unsullied white, coifed to right below the shoulders in a manner
that assured she kept a professional stylist on a hefty retainer. As
I got closer, I amended that to an entire professional salon on
salary. Her white linen dress reminded me of Marilyn Monroe.
She filled it out in a way that would have made even the first
supermodel jealous. A tan, lean leg stretched from an ivory
spiked high heel to a slit in her dress just before her thigh. If she
had been handcuffed, I would've thought she was a very
expensive hooker.

"If she was handcuffed, I'd ask how much."

As soon as that thought crossed my mind, she looked over at me. I blushed, half-afraid that she had heard my lusty inner voice. The embarrassment turned to confusion as I realized my escorts were marching me directly to her. Within moments of arriving next to her, the officers scattered as if whatever she or I had was highly contagious.

"Mr. Fisher." Her accent was vaguely continental. "I am glad you are finally free. Will you forgive me for taking so long in liberating you?"

I accepted her manicured hand and bowed to gently kiss her knuckles. "Of course, I didn't even realize I had a lawyer. Somehow I doubt you're a public defender."

Her laughter was rich and throaty. "No, you're quite right. My employer instructed me to fetch you." She whispered conspiratorially in my ear. "There's not enough money in the world to get me to defend some of these parasites…or to get me in handcuffs if I don't want to wear them."

I pulled back at that and looked her over again. She was flawlessly beautiful. Her skin was a creamy olive color that no spray or tanning bed could ever imitate. Her eyes and lips shimmered a ruby plum. I simultaneously wanted her and wanted to be nowhere near her. Had she heard my thoughts? I doubted it, but ….

"I'm sorry," she purred. "I can be a little forward. I hope I haven't offended you."

"No, no, you haven't. I just…I had thought of you in handcuffs before we ever spoke and your comment caught me off guard. Great first impression on my part. Colin Fisher, horny pervert."

She wrapped her arm around mine. "Duchess Deluce. Shall we get out of here or are you going to proposition me in front of all these officers of the law?"

There was something about her that suggested she was used

to getting what she wanted from men with a whisper, a purr, and an arm-wrap. That was enough to make me want to go the other direction just to prove a point. "I'd love to, but I've got to find out what they did with my car."

"Already taken care of. It's being towed from impound to an auto shop. I can provide our transportation until she's ready."

"Oh. Thank you, Miss Deluce, but I don't know that I can afford a mechanic."

We started walking toward a series of glass doors leading out to the street. "As I said, it's already taken care of. My employer gave me a healthy budget for this task and there's plenty extra since I didn't have to post bond for you or bribe any public officials. And, please, call me Duchess."

"She corrected the name, but not the 'miss' part. Jackpot."

"Hush, you. There's clearly been some kind of mistake. I don't have any friends rich enough to hire her to help me. We'll be nice, meet her employer. And once he figures out I'm not the guy he thought I was, I'll offer to pay him back out of my inheritance...assuming I haven't been formally disinherited."

When I looked up, we were standing beside a Lincoln MKX, a uniformed driver holding the door open for us. Duchess was staring at me, her head tilted to one side as if she were confused. I smiled and made a sweeping gesture into the vehicle. "After you, Duchess."

As she bent over to get in the car, I duplicated the spell I had used at the store last night, imagining an eggshell-white protective layer all over. I don't know why I did, but somehow I felt naked next to her.

"I can't imagine why you'd associate her and nudity. Really, not a clue."

5

Why the dinner date remained popular was a mystery to me. Most of the foods I preferred were difficult, if not impossible, to eat while projecting an aura of *savoir-faire* at the same time. It was even worse when the female half of the date was so obviously out of my league. Fortunately, I was starving and my survival instinct vetoed any desire to impress my lawyer.

Duchess had suggested a place called the Petroleum Club, but I stood firm. I didn't want to run up the tab any higher than I had to until I actually met her mystery employer. She had assured me a few thousand here or there wouldn't faze him. I then played my trump card and said that after only two candy bars and bean paste in the last day, I didn't think I could wait for a kitchen to prepare anything. Consequently, Duchess was the most elegantly dressed woman to ever sit in a McDonald's booth.

"So when do I get to meet this boss of yours?" I asked between monster-sized bites.

She slurped from her strawberry milk shake. "Tomorrow morning. He's flying in from Boston."

I laughed. "You've never been awkward a day in your life,

have you?"

She glanced around nervously, as if the décor might attack her. "What? Is there …?"

"No, I mean you looked mortified when your straw made that noise. Have you ever even eaten fast food before?"

"Is it that obvious?" She shook her head and returned my laughter in kind. "I haven't giggled like this in ages. You…I can't predict you." She slurped loudly, this time on purpose. "So, client-to-lawyer…did you kill any of them?"

"Are you sure that's a burger-and-fries type of question?" I glanced around to make sure no one else was listening. "And how many is 'them'? The FBI wasn't particularly specific as to how many bodies I was supposed to have racked up."

"Six in the last month. All frozen, all mutilated. The police are getting desperate. Be glad I showed up or you'd still be stuck in there, sixth body or no sixth body. And you didn't answer me. Did you kill any of them?"

"No." I shook my head.

"But you've killed someone before?"

"No…I don't know."

"Yes."

Duchess winced as if she had an air horn go off next to her ear. I put my hand on hers. "Are you okay?"

"That's the second time something like that has happened. Let me try something."

"What are you up to?"

"Just keep talking to her and stealing glances at her chest. I'll handle the rest."

"Duchess…are you all right?"

She shook her head, looking very far from all right. She stole a swig of my Dr. Pepper. "Headache, I think, nothing too …."

"GET OUT OF MY HEAD!"

She stopped in mid-sentence, her cheeks paling till they were the same tint as her hair. "All right, all right, I'll behave," she said weakly.

I nibbled my fries contemplatively. "You're a telepath."

She nodded. "I barely even think about it anymore. Most people practically broadcast what they're thinking. You...your defenses are impressive."

I tried my shielding spell again, adding a helmet-shaped bubble covering my head. "Be careful when delving into the affairs of wizards for they are subtle and quick to steal your French fries. I may be misquoting." I waited another second. "Is that better?"

"I'm out, Girl Scout's honor. I can shut it down when I have to."

"Murder, telepathy, and handcuffs. Definitely not the usual first dinner conversations. Most people would have run away screaming long ago."

She snaked one golden strand of crisp potato between her luscious lips. "I'm not most people. Unseelie fey blood on my mom's side."

Now it was my turn to look shocked. "Seriously?"

"Yeah, what about you? You're clearly not human."

I didn't know how to answer. "As far as I know, yeah, I am. I have been studying magic ever since ...."

"Totally human, absolutely. Nothing to see here, move along."

When I didn't finish, she picked up where I left off. "Since when? I've met a few wizards and most of them are as easy to read as anyone else. Fakers and shakers."

"Since...you asked me if I ever killed someone. I haven't. At least I don't think so. I had this fiancée in college, Sarai. I loved her like crazy. She worked in a bookstore off campus. I must have bought a hundred extra books just as an excuse to see her. It took a while, but she gave in. We had a year together. One wonderful year...and then she was gone. She had spent the night in my apartment. We stayed up late reading spooky stories and munching popcorn. When morning came, she had simply disappeared. I...it changed everything."

Duchess rubbed her hand on top of mine. "Let me guess. You spent all your time looking for her instead of going to class. You saw her everywhere, but it was never really her. Losing a love sucks, believe me, I know. But you didn't kill her. And how did it get you into magic?"

"Maybe I did kill her. I have trouble remembering that night. And...the door was still chain-locked in the morning. Either she jumped out of a fourth-floor window, walked through a wall, or she never left the apartment."

"You ate her. Every last drop."

Duchess leaned back and closed her eyes. She tightened her face in an effort of concentration. "I believe you, Colin. I'm going to tell him that you didn't kill any of his employees. I'm also going to tell him to hire you. If he offers you a job, any job, I suggest you take it."

"Is that why he sprung me out of jail? A job offer?"

Her smile was melancholy. "No. He wanted you free so he could torture and kill you himself. He's not happy that someone is picking off his employees. And when he's not happy ...." Duchess shuddered all over.

6

I called home to Uncle James and Aunt Celia that night before going to bed. It was awkward and difficult.

My sleep was restless for the rest of the night. I blamed it on the soft mattress at the hotel. I had gotten so used to sleeping in the car or under the stars that a real, honest-to-goodness bed gave me bad dreams. Thinking about murder all day might have had something to do with it as well.

In my mind's eye, I could see Sarai, curled up into a ball at the end of that hideous paisley couch I had back in college. Her feet were tucked underneath her, her arms wrapped around her knees, her teeth absentmindedly digging into her lower lip. I'm reading a story from the book, that cursed, vile tome I threw into the fire years ago. Every word terrifies her, tantalizes her, the fear and the passion all tangled up together inside of her. Sarai loved to be scared.

In the dark recesses of that ancient cavern,
I could hear the mad priest still chanting,
His deathless voice repeating the forbidden words,
Fast and frantic, an insane jumble of ranting;

Yog-Shoggoth Abishai Nostaru Nofar Immi-shoggoth.
Yog-Shoggoth Abishai Nostaru Nofar Immi-shoggoth.

Then, she is next to me, her face nuzzled up against mine. She kisses me, her lips seeking deep purchase in mine. Her taste is salty, metallic…bloody from where she bit her lip. She pulls back from me with a mischievous grin. "Blood of a virgin. Better be careful."

"You know we could fix that. No mad priest could use you for a sacrifice if you weren't a virgin."

"Mmm. I suppose you'd chant over me as we made love."

"Only if you wanted me to."

She pulls back into her story-time position. "Finish the story. If I like the way it ends, maybe you'll get lucky."

"Let's see, where was I …?"

Yog-Shoggoth Abishai Nostaru Nofar Immi-shoggoth.
Yog-Shoggoth Abishai Nostaru Nofar Immi-shoggoth.
Each syllable of that dark tongue echoed
Over water and stone and I knew then what must be done.

When I pause to turn the page, it is no longer Sarai on the couch with me, but Agent Devcreaux. "We found my body, you know." She pulls off her t-shirt to reveal the bloody cavity between her breasts. "Why? Why did you kill me?"

"Blood of a virgin. How could I have known?"

I hear Duchess' voice whisper in my ear. "You're clearly not human. You ate her. Every last drop."

I dreamed that same dream with slight variations five times that night. In the worst of them, she made love to me while I stared at the hole where her heart should have been.

7

The chauffeur delivered me to an IHOP six blocks from the hotel. I got quite the assortment of looks in the parking lot. I wondered whether it was my jeans, t-shirt, and leather jacket contrasting with my transportation or the fact that it was a limo in front of a pancake restaurant. I suspected most of them craned their necks to see whose bodyguard I was. Duchess wasn't with me, so the celebrity gawkers had to be disappointed.

I happily noted Dorothy's presence in the parking lot, her silver hood shining under a fresh coat of wax. I took good care of her, but she looked fit for royalty after Duchess' people got through with her. Whoever she worked for, he didn't believe in doing things halfway. Assuming there was a new battery to go with the makeover, I would have to sincerely thank him.

"Unless he also wired a bomb to her ignition. Don't forget he sent Duchess to kill us," my inner voice was kind to remind.

"Only if I was guilty. And he wanted to kill me himself. If you're going to spew paranoid conspiracy theories, at least keep your facts straight."

The restaurant was mostly empty. The senior citizen early birds had finished their meals, while the late morning brunchers were still packing their kids off to school. Kids were still going to school, right? It was mid-October, but I didn't have a clue what day of the week it was. Windowless cells have that effect on a lot of their residents, but I wasn't much of a calendar and appointment book guy before that. Thursday, I decided. It felt like a Thursday.

It wasn't hard to pick out Duchess' boss. For starters, he could have purchased ownership of the restaurant for substantially less than what he had spent on his black designer suit. It had been tailored to his unique frame, lending him an air of grace and sophistication, while still providing hints of the iron muscle underneath. A white Nero-collar shirt with silver buttons contained his large neck and bulging chest. His black hair was neatly trimmed, every wisp held in place by a veneer of hair spray. Beyond his well-coifed exterior, however, he radiated a commanding aura. I doubted any lesser mortal could be called "boss" by Duchess Deluce.

As I showed myself to his table, I tried to relax my vision to look through him. An old herb woman in Oregon had taught me how to see auras, a talent I didn't practice nearly as often as I should have. I pretended I didn't do it often because it was an invasion of privacy, but the truth was that it was too much like work. It was hard on the eyes to let loose of my focus, but it was even harder if what I saw forced me to take action. I can't see someone depressed, in pain, or haunted by a spiritual parasite and not try to help. Deep down, I have the heart of a knight. Like most knights, I'd had the crap kicked out of me more often than I could count for sticking my nose where it didn't belong. Both dragons and damsels can be equally resentful of outside interference, no matter how well intentioned.

However, meeting a fae-blooded telepath reminded me that I was part of a much larger universe. If pressed, I called myself a wizard, but that was only out of convenience. I couldn't throw a fireball or call lightning out of a cloudless sky, but I was capable of things that would make even the most cynical atheist pause. Most of my magic fell into one of three distinct categories: Foresight, Chance, or Emotion. Aura sight was part of the first and mostly involved convincing my conscious brain to shut up long enough for me to hear how my unconscious brain viewed the world. If Duchess' boss was anything other than human...

But human was all he was. His aura blurred in around the edges, but looked much like any other essence. I briefly closed my eyes to get a better feel for the color by contrasting it against the back of my eyelids. Most auras have a rainbow assortment of colors with band thickness and distance from the body telling the story of the person's current internal state. His revealed only a granite gray shell, the outside layer concealing all else. It was human, but it was disciplined human. He either meditated regularly or was using something akin to my eggshell shield spell. The choice of color, cold, hard, and unyielding, spoke volumes about the man.

"Mr. Fisher. Sit, please." His voice fit both the outfit and the aura. I thought I heard a slight Boston accent on the r's, more "ah" than "er". I did as he asked, taking up residence in the booth across from him.

With a gloved hand, he produced an ivory white business card and slid it across to me. In silver letters, "Lucien Valente" had been embossed in the center of the card. No phone numbers, titles, or e-mail addresses cluttered it; only his name appeared. While I inspected it, he removed the glove before grabbing a piece of toast off his plate and holding it out to me. "Take, eat."

"Do this in remembrance of me?" I added.

"Something like that. I know many of your kind regard guest right as important. It's not...kosher to harm someone you've shared a meal with."

I nodded. "Many Arab tribes believe it makes men family until the next sunrise. Refusing to eat is almost an act of war." I accepted the bread and took a nibble. "I hope you don't mind if I order my own plate for the rest."

He smiled, but said nothing until after our waitress came and left. I ordered a coffee, a tall stack of pancakes, fried eggs, and hash browns. I was on his tab, I assumed, and I was never one to skimp on a free meal. It's like the twelfth law of wizarding, I think.

"Colin Fisher." He rolled my name around on his tongue. "Do you know who I am?"

"Lucien Valente?" I ventured.

He nodded.

"Never heard of you before…though I must say I'm impressed so far."

"Are you familiar with Valente International?"

I racked my brain for a moment. "Big multinational conglomerate. Owns that coffee chain and the dollar discount stores."

"Among other things. I like to keep my interests diversified. I also don't care for advertising my success. Bill Gates, I'm not."

I let out a low whistle. I had friends in environmental movements who liked to go on long rants about the evils of multinationals. The more I thought about it, the more I recalled Valente International been spoken of in a tone of voice generally reserved for topics such as Nazis or terrorists. "That Lucien Valente, huh?"

"Yes, Mr. Fisher." He paused for a sip of his coffee. I noticed he drank it black, a trait I associated with strong character and honesty, probably because it matched my own preference. "Miss Deluce seems to think I should hire you on as my personal wizard. Was that her idea or yours?"

"Hers. I didn't know who her boss was. And Duchess didn't

strike me as someone whose opinion could be pushed around or manipulated. If she says she thought of it, she must have."

"No," he conceded. "She is an exceptionally stubborn secretary." I must have cocked an eyebrow in surprise, because he responded to my body language. "Yes, secretary, executive assistant, whatever the in-fashion term is. She provides external order to my life and activities, and acts in my stead when I am otherwise engaged. I believe the archaic term suits her better: she is my seneschal."

We sat in silence after that. My breakfast arrived and I began to eat. I could tell Lucien was waiting for something, but I didn't have a clue what. So I attended to what I did understand: blueberry syrup atop hot golden pancakes.

I was four or five bites in when Lucien started to laugh. "I give up, Mr. Fisher. I've had twelve other personal wizards before you. Most were con artists or one-trick ponies. Near worthless. But I think I like you."

I had enough etiquette to swallow before replying. "Why's that?"

"You're not trying to impress me. No dire prophecies of doom or demonstrations of power. You don't need to. That's the sign of real power, isn't it? When you don't feel the need to show it off, it means you really have it."

"I know a little," I confessed. "Enough to know that I'm not the biggest fish in the sea. But my luck and love spells pack a mean punch." My last luck spell, in fact, had accidentally killed its recipient. He won a quarter million dollars on the roulette wheel before karma straightened itself out in the form of a speeding bus. After that, I was very careful to limit my scope when I tinkered with probability. None of that seemed particularly interview-relevant, however. Scratch that. It probably was interview-relevant, but I suddenly wanted to get this job and thought that anecdote might sour the deal.

"Ooh, ooh, tell him about the couple on their honeymoon you put in the nuthouse. I love that story."

"Hmm." He proceeded. "What about curses? Do you know how to break them?"

"Depends on how it got there in the first place. It can be as simple as getting the person who placed it to unspeak the curse or as complex as paying reparations." All of which I understood in theory. I was well read in virtually every field of magic. In practice, however, I had never seen a real curse in action. From what I had studied, that was part of how curses operated: they blended into the background, subtly tilting reality toward their destination.

"This one is not simple, but perhaps some form of reparations could be made. I'm afraid I don't know who placed it on me."

"I see." I chewed it over, along with a mouthful of egg. "I'd have to study it, then. How do you know you've been cursed?"

He held up a hand. "We'll get to that, if I hire you. Breaking it will be your first professional duty. Could you do it?"

I should have insisted on more details or revealed my inexperience in the curse-breaking arena. But the truth was I was enjoying eating in restaurants, sleeping in hotels, and not worrying about how to pay for it. I was a good vagabond, but I knew I couldn't live that life forever. So I lied. "Of course I can."

"Sure, you'll lie to a murderous, powerful lord of capitalism, but not to the FBI about a little thing like murder."

His steely blue eyes dug into me. After a minute, he leaned back in his seat. "I think you can. I really do."

"Is this the part of the interview where I ask what your company does and what my responsibilities will be?"

"Valente International maintains form and balance in a world determined to plunge into chaos. It makes me money in the process, but I assure you it also serves humanitarian interests, the greater good. I'm what you might call the Devil You Know. I may be evil, but I keep much worse things at bay. I make sure there's a food store and coffee shop every other block. I don't like it when people disappear or families get slaughtered in their homes, because the dead and the abducted can't spend money or work jobs. I want you to know that up front, Colin Fisher. I am evil, but I'm your evil. I uphold society and, in turn, society upholds me."

"Your honesty is refreshing." I tried not to shudder. "Drugs? The meth they found on the clerk, he was selling that for you?"

"A subsidiary of a subsidiary of a subsidiary, I assure you. In a perfect world, I would only peddle pot. Ice makes people dangerous, unpredictable. But he was an employee, regardless, and I take his murder as a personal insult."

"So you're like the mob?"

His smile was predatory. "No, I'm a businessman. But legalities don't define the limits of my enterprise. Again, I'm the Devil You Know. If I didn't handle it, others, less pleasant than me, would. Have you seen the news coming out of Juarez or Tijuana?"

"Point well taken," I said. "But I've already got the FBI interested in me. I'm not sure crime would be the best career move for me."

"I'm aware of the bureau's interest in you. Your job tasks need not delve into the more illicit activities connected to me. My personal wizard answers only to me and handles three responsibilities. First, I need you to advise me regarding the supernatural. Second, I have agreements with the fae courts, a truce of sorts. You will act as my emissary in any such matters. Third, you will protect me from the magic of my enemies. There are plenty of people out there who think they can do the job better than I can, and I'm certain the serious contenders have personal wizards as well. In exchange for performing these services, you will have access to my Inner Circle, the resources of my various enterprises, and …" He slid an envelope across the table. "A healthy paycheck."

I pulled out the cashier's check and tried to keep a straight face. "This is my annual salary?" I hoped I sounded nonchalant about it, but doubted it.

"Annual? No, Mr. Fisher, that should cover the first week."

I whistled at that.

"Besides…of my last dozen wizards, only one lasted longer than a month."

8

I should have politely, very politely, asked permission to leave, gotten in Dorothy, and driven until her tank was empty. But the check in my hand was a heavy anchor holding me in place. Ultimately, I blame what happened on my ego. I had too high of an opinion of myself to really believe that I could fail him. And so I stayed in my seat, contemplating the six digits printed on the check. Let me be clear: six digits, decimal point, two zeroes.

"Two conditions," I added, once I thought I could trust my voice. "If you ask me to do anything I find morally repugnant or illegal, I can say no."

"You would turn down my offer over ethics?"

I took a deep breath. "Yes, I would."

He nodded. "The condition is acceptable. I dislike getting my hands dirty as well. I will not force you to do anything you deem immoral. Your second condition?"

He caught me off guard. I had expected that one to be a deal breaker. "Two...I want your help with a personal issue. I want you to use your resources to find a girl. Sarai, she's ...."

"I'm familiar with the strange case of Miss Claremore. I rarely step into anything blind, Mr. Fisher. I take it, then, you didn't kill her."

"No, I didn't." My personal uncertainties and dark doubts didn't need to be aired out in front of Valente.

"My resources are yours in the matter, though I would ask that you concentrate on the curse first." He paused for emphasis. "The job is yours, Mr. Fisher. Will you accept it?"

"Let me help out here. Y-E-S."

I really disliked it when my shadow and I agreed on something. It was usually a sure sign I was about to make a humongous mistake. "I'm your wizard." Pause. "Might I ask why? What makes you want to hire me?"

"I could give you a number of reasons. First, I think you could say no to me. Yes men are cheap and readily available; character is not. Second, you impressed Miss Deluce and she is not easily taken in. However, the most decisive factor is that there is something about you I do not wholly understand, a numinous element, if you will. I have survived a long time in a perilous business by using people who can do what I cannot. Be it fae-blood, gypsy-blessed, or demon-spawn, I employ the supernatural when I see it. If it won't work for me, I make peace with it…or I kill it."

I gulped. I doubted his backup plan for me included peace talks. "What don't you understand about me?"

"You managed to shut out Miss Deluce. According to her, you are the only human ever to catch her in the act and force her out. That alone is remarkable; even my own discipline is not flawless against her and I have the advantage of knowing what she is capable of. You also managed to survive the curse once, which is what initially caught my attention. I thought perhaps you were a part of the curse at first."

Curse? I really hoped he wasn't saying what I thought he was. "The attack at the gas station?"

"Yes."

"But curses are subtle. They bend probability. That was ...."

"A nightmare, yes. But I assure you, it is a curse. I received a letter in the mail six months ago. The letter never should have been able to make its way to my hand, but it did." Lucien produced a manila envelope and handed it me. "The postmark was from Oklahoma City."

The top page inside was a photocopy of the letter. I scanned it over, feeling the hairs on the back of my neck rise as I read. It was written in a feminine, cursive script. The occasional tremor suggested the writer was either very old or very emotional. The word "curse" was used ten times. I suspected that was important. Repeated words and number patterns generally mean things in magic. The writer didn't specify why she was cursing Lucien Valente beyond the most general accusations ("You take, you take, you consume until nothing is left").

The last line made me shudder as I recalled the store room of the gas station: "I curse you with the Winter, heartless Winter, a hunger greater than your own."

"That sounds vaguely familiar."

"You think she is doing this?" I hesitated, then added, "How many have died?"

"Six. The pace is quickening. Three months passed between the first two attacks. There was less than a day between the last two."

"Winter is coming," I commented, mostly to myself. "Whatever she did, it's only going to get stronger, more vicious, as we get closer to true winter." I wanted to add, "If the curse is magic and not a demented psychopath," but in that moment I knew. No serial killer could quick-freeze a person like that. There might be chemicals that could do it, but they would be easily traceable, the sort of work modern police detectives are best at. The detectives hadn't yet arrested the villain; ergo, it wasn't within their domain. It was magic – a heartless Winter curse. Worse, I had already volunteered to fight it.

"I suspect as much, but magic is not my forte. You survived it, so you are the expert."

"The clerk died while I was in the store? I felt a presence, but …."

"So it would seem," Lucien said. "The temperature change has given the coroner fits, but on the surveillance video, the employee went into the back mere seconds before you entered the store."

I thought back to how cold the fridge handle had been, and my snap decision to go with coffee rather than soda. Had the curse been waiting behind the door, waiting to pounce? I muttered, "It's not mature yet."

"Yes, you already said as much."

"No, I said it was getting stronger. This…this curse isn't full grown yet. It needed the cold of the coolers to make it powerful enough to kill. It was scared to come out into room temperature."

"Not even through the crime scene reports and already you see the common thread." Lucien smiled. "There was a source of ice at each crime scene."

I flipped past the letter and saw the rest of what he had given me in the envelope. Every report, every crime scene photo, even hand-scribbled detective notes were in my hands. "How did you get this?"

He shrugged. "Not everyone is as moral as you."

I glanced over it all, moving quickly past the photographs. "It didn't like it when I cast my shield spell. I think it was waiting for me behind the door until then. The air was so cold. But it felt the energy moving, my magic, and decided to run." My mind returned to the first call afterward. "It growled, tried to run me off, to mark its territory. It's getting stronger, but it still doesn't like the idea of a straight up fight. Were there elements of an ambush at each scene? The victim had just turned a corner or opened a door, something like that?"

He nodded, though his face was puzzled. "Growled?"

I told him about the thing panting over the phone and the ancient language I couldn't quite place. For reasons involving straitjackets and psychotropic medications, I had left that part out of my police interviews.

Lucien Valente sat pensively, slowly working away at his coffee. After a lengthy pause, he said, "Tell me what it all means."

I had been mulling it over in my own mind in the silence. I had an idea, but was I on the right track?

"It's plausible. But ...."

"But what?"

"If that is what's going on, then it's not immature or getting stronger. It's waking up. And that's bad news. The last time one came out of hibernation was 1846 and that was just long enough to wipe out eighty percent of a wagon train."

"The Donner party?"

Yeah. But that was just a midnight snack. For all intents and purposes, it rolled over and went back to sleep once its belly was full.

"But this one is awake." I flipped back to the letter. *"Somebody went poking at it with a stick until it was up and moving."*

"And it's not going back to sleep until it's destroyed Valente International...if even then."

"Why wouldn't it once the curse was fulfilled?"

"Colin, there's a reason the spirit speakers didn't call on them when the white man started stealing their land. Their people had to go to war to force them into slumber. If it gets fully awake, nothing short of a war is going to knock it back out. As soon as it gets done with the curse, my guess is it will go after the people that woke it up, followed by anybody around with enough magical juice to be a threat to it."

"How did you learn so much about this stuff? I don't remember ever reading about an ancient Native American spirit war."

"Just because you want to believe I'm part of your subconscious don't make it so, kemosabe."

"Mr. Fisher?" There was no sound of impatience in Lucien Valente's voice, but I suspected I had been talking to myself for far longer than I had intended to.

"Wendigo. In Native American lore, it's a cannibal spirit of the frozen north. It gained power by counting coup...umm, eating a part of those it defeats. It's usually pictured as either a dire wolf or a winter storm. There are two possibilities. Either the woman sending the curse woke up a real wendigo or she's drawing power on the wendigo myth to enhance a lesser spirit or thought form."

He held up a hand. "I don't need the technical details, Mr. Fisher. I am convinced you know what you are talking about." The waitress came back and Lucien paid the check before he spoke again. "You're proving more enlightening than my last wizard already. He wouldn't even admit that it was definitely supernatural."

"Speaking of which, what happened to him?"

"Miss Deluce didn't tell you?" Valente shook his head as if this neglect amused him. "You owe your freedom to the man, incompetent though he was. While you were being questioned by the police, the wendigo ate him."

SECOND INTERLUDE

S pecial Agent Andrea Devereaux of the Behavioral Sciences Investigative Division didn't dare to pull her head away from the sink long enough to investigate anything. The coughing was subsiding, but she still felt like she had been gargling pond water all morning long. When she was confident she didn't have anything left to spit out, she poured a shot of Listerine and swished it around with a sense of determined desperation.

The trip to Oklahoma was not her favorite expedition with the BSID. She had been looking forward to a trip to the pumpkin patch with her nieces this weekend in New York, not a gruesomely weird case in Oklahoma. Picking up and leaving at the drop of a hat came with the territory of hunting serial killers and rapists. Andrea had dreams of becoming the FBI's first female director and the BSID was a good career path for her to use to get there. But Oklahoma was making her seriously rethink her life's direction.

The crime photos had been nasty, but not the worst she had ever seen. The trouble didn't really start till they got to the lake to investigate the suspect's vehicle. Andrea usually had a sharp memory, but she could barely recall the lake at all. A thick fog had settled over that part of her brain. When she tried, all she could think of was that thick leather bound book…and the terror that it conjured inside of her. It was insane to think that decorated Special Agent Devereaux could be scared of a book, but that one particular tome ….

She must be getting sick. That was the simplest explanation: some bad food on the plane or an armrest she should have sanitized, but didn't. But agents didn't let illness interfere with their job. Andrea had absolutely bombed the interview with the suspect, Colin Fisher. Her questions, or what she could remember of them, had been all over the place. Without plan, without direction, Fisher had easily stayed ahead of her. He had gotten away with murder once from all indications…and her sickness was helping him do it again.

She stared long into the bathroom mirror after she spewed out the mouthwash. Her hazel eyes, a mixture of brown, green, and gold stared back at her, the same as they had from every mirror for as long as she could remember. Andrea hoped that whatever had gotten into her system was out of it now. She needed to be at her very best for the rest of this investigation.

PART THREE

FAERIES, COWORKERS, AND WENDIGOES, OH MY!

"Finding a dragon is usually the easy part, just follow the path of razed towns and smoldering farms. The hard part comes after you catch up to her."

-Jadim Cartarssi, Novice Dragonslayer

1

I expected to have difficulty cashing Valente's check. As it turned out, that was the easiest thing I did all day. All of my past experience with banks told me that an out-of-state driver's license plus no personal account plus a check of that magnitude would equal nothing but trouble. It had started out that way, too...until the branch manager made one phone call. From the speed and grace he demonstrated after he hung up, I decided the bank must have belonged to a subsidiary of Valente International. In less than twenty minutes, I had ten grand in my pocket, along with a debit card electronically linked to the rest of it. I just hoped that the dead wouldn't start asking to borrow money from me while I was trying to work the ATM.

Duchess was supposed to meet me at my hotel room the next morning with the items I had requested from Lucien, most notably, the original letter. I've had a little practice with psychometry and, in theory, the letter could be used as a magical tether tracing back to the person who wrote it. It was a Foresight task and I was reasonably proficient with those. It was the theoretical part that bothered me. I knew enough to connect the attacks with the idea of a wendigo, but I had never seen one, let alone killed one.

"Good thing it's only killing Valente employees…oh, wait."

"I didn't hear you telling me not to take his check."

"That was before I knew it was going to involve actual work. I was hoping he had been cursed with erectile dysfunction or something lame like that. You know, burn some incense, slip some Viagra in his Kool-Aid, chant a little and call it a day."

"Yeah, well, we're stuck now. I don't suppose you have any neat anti-wendigo tricks to go along with your telepathic countermeasures and knowledge of secret Indian spirit wars?"

"Never met one. I guess we'll see when we come nose to snout. You know, we could …."

"No."

"But you didn't even let me finish," my inner voice complained.

"I'll finish for you. No. I'm not using the Necronomicon to conjure up something to fight it. Nine times out of ten, I'd end up with something worse than a wendigo at the end of the day."

"But we know it works. The rest of your magic has always been a little bit shaky. And we wouldn't have to bring something here. We could just open a rip in space and time and suck the wendigo through."

"And what happens if I can't close the rip back up and a tentacle or two comes slithering on out? No. Not unless all else fails."

"Fine. But I'm going to kill you if we become wendigo chow."

I needed to come up with a game plan. I'd have to learn everything I could about wendigoes (wendigi, wendigoose…let's stick with wendigoes). I was in an unfamiliar city, against a foe I'd only read about in stories, pretending to be a professional wizard. Oh, and the FBI still thought I was a serial killer in the making. Harry Potter I was not.

I started with the only thing I could think to do. I grabbed a phone book and checked under "Native American." I don't know what I was hoping for, but there were no shamans, raindancers, or medicine men listed in the yellow pages. There was a listing for a Red Dirt Native American Museum and Cultural Center. It sounded as promising a place as any to start, so I wrote down the address. On a lark, I flipped to "Wizard", but no one was brave enough to advertise as such. In L.A., Chicago, or New York, maybe, but apparently I was the only professional wizard in Oklahoma City.

My first difficulty came in buying a map of the metro area. When I started driving as a teenager, all I had to do was stop at any gas station and they'd have three different versions for whatever city I was in. If the station was near the Interstate, there would undoubtedly be a state map, plus another one for the nearest neighboring state. This made good business sense—everybody gets lost from time to time. Apparently, paper maps were going the way of the dodo and the typewriter. The first two store clerks both told me about this great map app on their phone. Numbers three and four weren't as obnoxiously techno-savvy, but their stores didn't carry maps, either. A customer behind me in line said that she was addicted to her DumDum GPS or something to that effect. In an Internet age, my inability to use the web was becoming a serious drawback. In the myths, Merlin never had to deal with a demon-possessed messenger pigeon.

At the fifth convenience store, I finally found a paper road map of OKC. I was so delighted to get it that I didn't even mind fighting with the creases to fold it back up when I was done. However, with traditional map in hand, my second challenge was obvious: Oklahoma City is huge. It doesn't seem that way. It feels like a quaint, small country town, like Mayberry with more cowboy hats and a handful of skyscrapers. But in reality, it's one of the biggest cities in the world by total land area. It took me over an hour to drive from my hotel in Midwest City to the museum in Edmond. My only hope was that they didn't have a rush hour or travel time was going to eat up my entire day.

The museum itself was something of a disappointment. If I had gone there to learn about the contributions of Native Americans to modern society, it would have been a great educational experience. But I had wendigo and spirit wars on the brain. Unless using a flint knife proved to be the secret to killing a cannibal winter spirit, Red Dirt wasn't much help. I checked the calendar outside the cultural center. There was a lecture on Great Plains Rain Dances set for next Monday, but even that was a long shot. The rest of the schedule was more social than religious. The gift shop didn't have any relevant books, but I did pick up some animal figurines: a bear, a wolf, and an eagle. I didn't have any immediate use for them, but with magic I never knew when a good symbol would come in handy.

I was going about this the wrong way. I needed to talk to an expert, someone familiar with Native American cosmology. Unfortunately, finding one who would talk to me would take time, years maybe. Unlike the Indo-European traditions I was familiar with, the Native American mystics didn't feel the compulsion to put everything into writing. Being able to read all the archaic languages in the world didn't help if no one had ever written a book on the subject.

I needed a way in: an intermediary who knew the lay of the land but who understood my side of the street, too. I needed a spirit guide.

2

I t was after noon by the time I reached the occult shop. Even in the heart of the Bible Belt, there was a demand for witchcraft and the accompanying paraphernalia. Granted, Gaea's Treasures was far more family-friendly than some of the stores I'd visited in New Orleans or New York, but it was still decisively pagan.

I'm not Wiccan; I'm Catholic. Any time I start to talk about magic, people make the assumption that I don't believe in Jesus or that I'm into goat sacrifices. Don't get me wrong. I think Wicca is great. Anybody who really lives their life by the code "And do no harm," is probably a decent neighbor and a good human being. My standard was love God and love the person standing next to me, but I was the first to admit I didn't always hit the mark.

"Do you ever hit the mark?"

The Bible and magic aren't opposed. The original authors clearly believed magic was possible, so much so that they were very specific about what forms of sorcery were not allowable. As far as I can tell, I'm not permitted to invoke other gods, practice necromancy, conduct séances with the dead, brew poisons, or offer human sacrifice. That leaves me a whole lot of room to work with. There are even stories in the Bible about divination, transmutation, and animal magics. Within the bigger picture, though, it's all about love. Any magic must be practiced within the confines of love towards God, myself, and my fellow man. Again, I was not one hundred percent on the mark, but I tried, and I liked to think the Big Guy gave me credit for that. Most of the sins I struggled against were a lot more mundane than necromancy.

"Lust, for example. Do you have any idea what you could get a girl to do for half of what's in your wallet right now? What about five girls and all the money in the ATM?"

I ignored him and got back to my shopping. Gaea's Treasures had a homey feel to it, probably because the owners lived out of the back half of the building. The right wall was given completely over to glass jars stuffed full of herbs. The combined smell was pleasant but pungent, like plowing head first into a field of wildflowers. I skimmed through their offerings and knew I'd end up back at the herb counter. They had quite a few items I thought I might need before the business with the wendigo was all said and done.

Herbs were a must-have for any magical practitioner. Shamans have been working with plants for hundreds of thousands of years, allowing humanity to accumulate a wide knowledge of herb lore. Beside their chemical properties, most herbs have well-known associations with certain spiritual essences. Take the rose, for instance. Love and romance are nowhere in its molecular makeup, but they still embodied the romantic archetype. Unfortunately, herbs were not the friend of the vagabond wizard. My trunk held enough questionable smells without adding valerian root to the mix…and I dreaded traffic stops without carrying extra green leafy substances.

Consequently, I usually traveled with only a small stash of catnip and feverfew. Don't look at me like that. Catnip is well known for its soothing properties. And I like cats.

"Sad, but true. Why couldn't you be an animal hater like most serial killers?"

For what I planned, I needed a wider palette to work with. Summoning and the protection spells required by summoning were not my strong suit. Magic, at its heart, was about will and belief. Everything else (swords, staffs, athames, wands, altars, etc.) was basically props. In theory, I could perform any spell entirely within the confines of my psyche, the way I did my defensive shell. Unfortunately, most spells involved a lot more elements and could go really, really bad if things weren't perfectly precise. Trying to track more than about three details at a time was generally more than my imagination could handle. By using physical representations, instead of mental ones, it left my brain free to attend to other aspects of the magical working.

Of course, I could be full of shit. Most of my notable arcane achievements range between dubious successes and horrific backfires. I hear this is quite common for rookie wizards, which may explain why there are so few seasoned veteran wizards running around: unnatural selection in action. Any sane person would have called it quits long ago.

"Good thing we're a French fry short of a Happy Meal."

I breezed past the candle aisle wistfully, then reversed march as I realized two things. First, I had a room! A hotel room is, granted, not ideal for magic, but it would offer me privacy and a controlled environment if I wanted to try something complex. Second, my magical experimentation now had funding! I could buy every item in the store if I wanted to...on my first week's salary. I loaded up my arms with different colors, sizes, shapes, and scents of candles, then gave up and went back to grab a shopping basket.

The new books didn't offer anything wendigo-specific or eye-catching, but the used book section took a little longer to go through. Even in specialty stores, people didn't always realize just how rare a book they had sitting on a shelf, especially when it came to books in foreign languages. That's part of how I had survived on the road for so long with so little money. I would buy something like the Rhine faeries book for twenty bucks, read it, and when I was done find the right sort of place to sell it for what it was really worth. A third of my library in Dorothy's backseat was devoted to faeries, but an *Illustrated Catalog of the Fae* had one thing the rest of my books didn't: pretty pictures, full page and in color. It was the first thing I had seen which I immediately knew how I would use. I wedged it carefully into the basket amongst my horde of scented candles.

The clothing and jewelry section was new turf for me. In the past, I skipped over such places without a second thought. But now that I was a professional wizard with a major league salary, it might not hurt to be able to look the part when the occasion required. I got the feeling that Lucien employed a lot of powerful, dangerous individuals with abilities that could make Duchess' telepathy look downright secretarial. A little bling, plus a Wendigo kill, might go a long way in establishing my street cred. I didn't want my new coworkers to lump me in with the other con men and one-shot wonders who had held my position previously.

"And I thought I was cocky. You're already shopping for the victory party," my inner voice taunted.

"Power of positive thinking, right?"

"Sure. Wishing everything was nice and pretty and perfect has worked so well for us in the past."

3

After I picked my herbs, the total on the register made me wince out of habit. All totaled, the damage was less than a tenth of what I had in my pocket, but it was still more than I had spent in the last month. I tried to comfort myself that I could spend this much on a daily basis and it wouldn't even come close to my weekly salary...and it would take a month of nothing but rituals to use up all the supplies I bought.

I put on the silver moon-and-stars ring and tucked the silk handkerchiefs into my jacket pocket. The rest was patiently stacked away in a trio of paper bags by the older man behind the counter. His hair was white and frazzled, but all still there. If he had written a book in his youth, it was either on an antique typewriter or papyrus, I wasn't sure which. I thanked him for his help, a half-assed apology for how many times I had changed my mind while he was bagging the various leaves, roots, and powders for me.

I was trying to figure out how to balance all the packages in my arms when he spoke. His voice was rough as sandpaper; his tone slow and sleepy. "Son, do you want some advice?"

It caught me off guard. He had been friendly while I shopped: smiles, nods, and grunts that conveyed more than most people's sentences. But hearing him speak, I realized those were the first words he'd directed at me. "Why do you ask?"

"You look like you could use some. But advice don't do no good unless a person wants to hear it."

"Shoot."

He looked me in the eyes, a long, hard look, before he spoke again. "My wife and I have been running this shop for thirty years now. Most people come in here, they're looking for excitement, a curiosity. Others are simple folk, just wanting to keep their home and loved ones safe from the evil eye, or the boogeyman. The one thing both types have in common is they ask questions, 'What's this do?' 'What's that do?' You ain't asked squat. Means you know what you're doing."

"Or think you do, at least."

"I hope so, but I'm not so arrogant as to think I don't have lots to learn." I mentally noted that I just learned yesterday that there really are living, breathing people with fae blood in their veins.

"Uh-huh. I ain't gonna try and teach you. Best way to learn is by doing." He paused. "You're fixin' to do some summoning."

I nodded.

"Thought so based on the shopping list. Look, there's some weird stuff out there. They'll tell you all kinds of things, offer all sorts of power. They'll threaten, cajole, beg, demand. Just remember two things." He took a sip out of his chipped and stained coffee mug. "You sure you want to hear this?"

I smiled. "You certainly know how to bait a hook. Yes, I'd like to hear it."

His laugh came out as a heh. "I suppose. One, they can't make you do anything you don't want to do. That's where the whole devil-made-me-do-it excuse falls apart: he couldn't make you if it wasn't in your heart already. Two, no matter what you do, there's always a way back. As long as you're still breathing, there's still a way back. You understand?"

"You're talking about forgiveness."

"Something like that. The worst lie spirits like to tell you is that what's been done can't be undone. It's such a terrible lie, because it's partly true. The effects you have beyond you, the ripples in the pond, you can't take back. But inside of you…you can make it back if you want to."

4

The toxic fumes had largely dissipated from my hotel room, but I was still reluctant to go back in. If I went inside I would have to go through with the ritual...or admit I was chicken. Outside the room, I could pretend like I was going to attempt the summoning whenever I got around to it. I'd do it after dinner or after the movie or, whoops, I stayed out too late, guess I'll whip up a summons after breakfast. If I stepped back inside the room, I'd have to get around to it. The whole process was starting to scare the hell out of me.

After Gaea's Treasures, I stopped by one of those hardware mega-stores to pick up the rest of the ritual supplies I needed. Like the other props, a literal circle was not strictly required, but having one would free my mind up to concentrate on other details, like staying alive. For a summoning, I wanted something solid, permanent. Unfortunately, even temporary methods of marking a circle could be rough on rented hotel room carpet. I didn't want to have to apologize to the cleaning staff as they vacuumed up a ring of salt or sand, so I picked up a seven- by-seven roll of vinyl flooring and a can of silver paint. While my circle dried, I went out to an early dinner. I really could get spoiled by this whole regular eating out thing. On the road, my idea of supper was four slices of bread and a couple lumps of peanut butter.

The vinyl mat didn't want to lie flat, so I drafted the room's furniture into service. The bed wouldn't budge, so I put the table upside down on the mattress, while my ritual area occupied its section of floor space, held in place by two chairs, a lamp, and the nightstand. I needed to be careful how I moved, but I thought I had left enough room to work with.

Taking a deep breath, I tried to let my anxiety roll out of me with the exhale, then began. If this worked, the portable circle would be reusable, but the rest of the summoning markings would need to go. I used a set of black, red, blue, and green dry erase markers to trace my designs on to the mat. The outer circle would contain the entire spell, but a square, second circle, and a pair of intersecting triangles would help me trap the spirit, if anything actually showed up.

I've used fairies to help with magic before, invoking certain names and rhymes to help fuel my spells. This approach seemed to work reasonably well. I'd seen them before too, as colored aura spheres of light just outside the focus of my vision. I believed in fairies, as much as anyone could…but I'd never met one. My assumption was that they operated on a different frequency of reality, a parallel dimension. Maybe they were here a long time ago, but they'd retreated from the world with the rise of man. It was a nice, safe theory that allowed me to believe without wondering why I'd never really interacted with one.

Duchess inadvertently challenged that. If fae and humans could have kids, that meant they could have sex, right? That implied touch, sight, hearing, smell, taste: this dimension. I mean, intercourse is *not* a parallel dimension sort of activity, though I've heard women accuse men of treating it that way. So if a fairy and a human had a child together, even if it was generations ago, that meant that the fae could materialize in this world, if they wanted to. If I was going to be a personal wizard for one of the world's most powerful men, with fae court emissary in the job description, I wanted to be able to say I had actually met a fairy face to face. If I was really lucky, I could find one that knew a little about wendigoes, too.

The lines in place, I set a candle at the point of each triangle. I picked up the page I had torn loose from the encyclopedia, and set it down dead in the center. It had taken me a bit to select what kind of fairy I wanted to meet. I needed a spirit guide with insider knowledge of wendigoes, but a fae with that level of power was best saved for after I had a little practice. The pookas had been helpful in past luck and illusion workings, but I was not sure I wanted a conversation with one. Much of their mystical power was based on a mythic reputation for trickery, hyperactivity, and creativity. Trolls and elemental sprites seemed like a bad idea in a confined space that didn't belong to me. The sidhe were amazingly beautiful, but equally fearsome in their power. Calling out the heavyweight champs of the fey realm for my first bout would not be smart, even by amateur wizard standards of stupid.

The picture I settled on was a group portrait of thirteen furry creatures with bigger hands than heads, using wrenches, hammers, and a crowbar on the rear axle of a wooden carriage. Gremlins were notorious mischief spirits, but were pretty low in the fairy pecking order. Their penchant for mechanical malfunctions gave me an excuse for trying the summons beyond mere curiosity. If it worked, I'd ask the gremlin why telephones and Internet connections hated me so much.

"When it works. You've got to believe, Colin."

"When did you become a cheerleader?"

"Strictly self-preservation. If Lucien decides you suck as a wizard, I

don't think it will go well for me, either…so pass the pixie dust and the green Kool-Aid."

Good point, great confidence booster, glad we had this talk. Now I was worried about both the spell *and* my new boss killing me.

On top of the picture, I added a sprinkle of sugar and a dash of licorice leaf as attractor. In mythology, faeries don't mind trading with mortals, but they tend to get annoyed if people presume to order them around. Accordingly, I placed a seven-inch-long plastic toy car inside the square, but outside the inner circle and the triangles it contained. It struck me as the sort of thing a gremlin would like: no metal, but plenty of small, moving parts.

With the trade-bait in place, I checked over everything, making sure I didn't smear any of the lines while setting the trap. Satisfied that it was as ready as it would ever be, I stepped back away from it before dropping to one knee. Most books on meditation recommend using a familiar, comfortable position, such as the student pose or the lotus position. I've used both, but as a lifelong Catholic, I preferred genuflection. My brain equated it with spiritual activity. While kneeling, I said a short prayer and began the process of focusing my mind for magic.

Getting my breathing under control came first. I focused on each inhale and exhale until they were slow and regular, feeling as if I was breathing through my belly button instead of my mouth. When that became automatic, I turned my attention to my aura. Gradually, I pulled my essence into a tight, glowing ball in the pit of my stomach. I willed it up toward my throat and pictured it as the same brown color as the gremlin's fur in the book. I picked the throat chakra as the release point on instinct.

Ready, I rose and moved back in to my ritual area. I lit the six candles in a clockwise fashion. Slowly, purposefully, I spoke:

"Makers of mischief,

Genius of engineering,
Sneaker, breaker,
Tinker, fixer.
I call thee forth
Honoring the most ancient traditions.
Tinker, breaker,
Sneaker, fixer,
I call thee forth
To trade, to chat.
Breaker, fixer,
Sneaker, tinker,
I call thee forth
And name thee gremlin."

On the last syllable, I imagined the ball of energy turning into a cloud and riding out of me on the wind of my breath. As I let it loose, it danced down to the closest candle, then twisted its way clockwise around the six flames in a loose mud-colored smoke ring. The next moment could only be compared to an orgasm, though even that comes woefully short of complete description. Everything in me peaked at the same moment, then suddenly emptied as the magic burst forth from me and into the circle.

In the midst of my breath, a new shadow began to form, composed of spindly over-sized arms and tiny nubs for legs. Before I could get a good look, there was a sudden

BRRRINNKRRAK!

I turned to see where the noise came from, just in time to identify the handset of the hotel phone hurtling at me. The mouthpiece struck dead center on my forehead. My last conscious thought was of Sarai.

5

I see Sarai and yet I know it's not her, can't be her. Her long brown hair is pulled up in a bun, a few stray strands hanging down to dance across the ivory skin of her shoulders. She's wearing a toga of pale seafoam silk, held together by a pearl clasp. Her long, lithe fingers stroke across my temples, my head reclining on her lap. Her hazel eyes are loving, eager, as they gaze down into mine.

My body is speaking, but I barely recognize the emerging voice. It is deeper, purer, a baritone trumpet next to my normal tenor sax. "We could deal with the Faceless Ones in one strike. What few orphans survived would scatter to the ends of the worlds."

Not-Sarai's voice is patient, an alto feminine mate to my dream voice. "The elders were cast out for a reason. They cannot be trusted, my love."

"Bah," I counter. "The elder ones love destruction and chaos. I will give them the chance to rain it down one last time: a battle to end all war."

"You are too confident, my knight, my heart. Do you think

the elders will willingly return to the outer oblivion when they are done serving as your mercenaries?"

"No, my moon and stars, they will not." I rise from her lap to pluck a kiss from her lips. The vibrations of it rumble through my essence. "But I can force them to just the same. I will not open a gateway, but a transfer. I will go to the outer darkness so that I might hold their leash."

Not-Sarai shakes her head. "I know the plan. But is it not possible that they might try to outwit you, to snap their tethers?"

"Then I am lost and the worlds will be theirs again. But what other choice do we have? I will not let the Faceless win."

She frowns and my heart breaks at the sight. "We could …."

Knock, knock.

"What was that, my love?"

Knock, knock, knock.

6

When I woke up, I was acutely aware of three things. First, Sarai, the woman I still loved with all of my heart, was not in the room with me. Second, the sun was peeking in through the hotel windows, meaning I had lost a lot of time since the ritual's conclusion. Third, my head felt like I had been pounding cheap Russian vodka all night long. That thought faded as I remembered the exploding telephone shrapnel. I revised the statement to my head felt like I was getting pounded by a giant telephone monster all night long.

Knock, knock.

This time I placed the sound and forced myself to stumble up off the carpet and towards the door. It was only after I pulled it open that I wish I had checked to see who it was first. I might have brushed my hair or put some fresh deodorant on for Duchess Deluce. She looked stunning, a vision in freshly fallen snow-white. I felt like a vision in what that same snow would look like after a week in the gutter next to a dog-walking business.

She cocked a pure white eyebrow. "Mr. Fisher? Is this a bad

time?"

I tried to pretend I didn't hear undertones that implied I might have a drinking problem or worse. "No, no." I shook my head. "I just got done with a little ritual, that's all."

I gestured her in. We both got to view the aftermath of last night's magic together. I could only imagine what she thought. The table had been knocked off the bed, blocking access to the bathroom. The pillow I set the telephone on when I moved the nightstand was now a blackened crater of foam, one stray piece of telephone wire poking free of the wreckage. The vanity mirror had splintered from two separate impacts. In short, it looked like a bomb had gone off.

"A little ritual?" She chuckled. "Remind me I don't want to be on the receiving end of one of your big…what on Earth is that?"

Her voice shifted up half an octave. I had to maneuver around her too see what had caught her attention. Most of the designs on my ritual floor were buried under a sea of dried candle wax, though not a drop had crossed the outer silver circle. Sitting where I had left the toy car, partially embedded in wax, was the ugliest, most misshapen red and cream colored brick I had ever seen. As I knelt down to inspect it, I realized it was a conglomeration of telephone pieces merged with plastic car parts and held together by strips of pillowcase and shreds of glossy paper from the gremlin picture. I silently checked the circle for any still-active magical energies before breaking the plane. When I picked up the chimera phone, I half-expected it to fall to pieces on contact, but was surprised by its solid construction.

I turned it over, looking at it from six different angles before I was certain what it was. "It's my new cell phone."

Duchess' laugh was amplified by my already throbbing headache. When she finally stopped, she said, "Too much, Mr. Fisher, too much. You've convinced Lucien you may have a little talent, but a magical cell phone? There's no need to con me now."

I fixed my best irritated wizard glare on her. It stopped her laughter. Sometimes resembling Charles Manson comes in handy. "I bet you it works."

A lone giggle escaped, but her deeper laughter remained dammed. "If that thing can make a phone call, I'll ...."

"You'll what? Give me whatever I ask for?"

That stopped her humor altogether. "And if it doesn't, what do I get?"

I pulled my debit card and set it on the bed. "The rest of my paycheck."

"Hang on a second, champ. Phones and you aren't ...."

"No", she said firmly. "I have plenty of money. When it doesn't work, you have to lower your defenses. I get fifteen minutes inside your head, no resistance."

"No thanks. I'll pass."

"Deal." I started looking over the mishmash of buttons. The two and the eight were set like a pair of eyes on the head of the device, while the other buttons spiraled out in the belly. "What's your cell number?"

She grinned. "No. If your toy is magical, it should be able to figure it out on its own. I want you to call ..." She thought for a moment. "Veruca. Veruca Wakefield."

"Who is she?"

"A member of Lucien's inner circle. You get her on the phone, I'll know it's magic. I don't even have her cell number...just Valente."

I scratched my head. "You expect me to believe you don't know it? You're Lucien's secretary."

"That's why I picked her. Just in case you have some telepathic ability yourself. You'll find our employer is rather fond of his secrets." She moved closer, her hand going to my chest.

"Of course, if you're scared, I'll let you back out of the bet for only five minutes in your mind."

Coming from her lips, five minutes of mental rape almost sounded seductive. "I'll pass. I think you need to learn a little respect for the resident wizard."

I don't know why cynicism about magic from her bothered me. Most people I met were more than a little skeptical about my abilities. Heck, I was skeptical of my abilities most of the time. But I wasn't going to let someone with actual fae blood in her veins stand there and mock my magical prowess.

I stared down at my gremlin-assembled phone, contemplating the problem. I didn't know why I knew it would work. I had traded for it, paid for it with a toy car and a blow to the head. By the laws of the fae, it would work. If it didn't...well, maybe I was a charlatan after all.

With a sudden burst of insight, I punched the zero button and spoke into the mouthpiece. "Operator, connect me to Veruca Wakefield. Inner Circle of Valente International. Yes, that's W-A-K-E-F-I-E-L-D. Wakefield. I'll hold."

No one responded as I spoke, but I tried to hold up my end of an operator-assisted conversation as best as I could. The device burped and a speaker emerged from the tangled mess, slowly crawling its way up the side of my head toward my ear. There was no ringing sound, no dial tone, but there was something. A humming, perhaps, or a melody of bird songs heard miles and miles away. Duchess started to pace around me like a hungry tiger. But, true to my beliefs, a minute later I heard, "Wakefield."

I used my best professional sales voice. "Veruca Wakefield? Of Lucien Valente's Inner Circle?"

There was a brief pause. "Who the hell is this?"

"That depends. What do you think of Duchess Deluce?"

"That bitch," the voice growled.

"Oh, well, in that case, I'm the man you just helped win a bet against her. Name's Colin Fisher. I'm the new wizard."

The line went silent again. "What happened to Enrique what's-his-name?"

"Wendigo ate him."

"Too bad, he was kind of cute. Dumb, but cute. So…Colin. Since we haven't met yet, I'll pretend that you didn't know any better. Just tell me who gave you this number and I'll kill them instead." Veruca sounded feminine, almost valley girlish, yet she managed not to let her voice detract from the believability of the death threat.

"Sorry, a magician never reveals his secrets. Look, if I tell Duchess the words you used to describe her, will she believe that I really am talking to you right now?"

"You want her to know it's me, huh?" Miss Wakefield went on a profanity laden tirade that encompassed five different languages and expressed such heartfelt dislike that I expected my phone to melt. "Tell her that and she'll believe you."

I clucked. "Hmm. I'm not sure I'll survive the telling. If I tell her that, I should get something out of it."

"You get to live, how's that?"

"I was thinking more like a meal. Burger King, maybe? This whole eating out every day thing is still new to me."

A longer silence. "I threaten to kill you and your counter-offer is a date?"

"Well, it's not every day I meet a girl who can cuss better and make better death threats than me. Not to mention there's something about the Portuguese language off a woman's lips that drives me wild."

The longest silence yet. "Very well, Colin. If you tell Duchess that, word for word, I will buy you a meal at Burger King."

I pushed the mouthpiece out of the way. "Miss Deluce, I apologize, but I am to deliver this from Miss Wakefield verbatim." I proceeded to do so, then raised the mouthpiece again, "Satisfied?"

"Eminently, though...you had the accent right on all the words. I may have to get you to swear at me if you're that practiced at it. Do you actually speak Korean?"

"When I have to."

"Hmm. Intriguing." The valley girl quality was gone from her voice. "Good day, Mr. Fisher."

"Good morning, Miss Wakefield."

The earpiece retracted itself, apparently sensing the call was over.

Duchess' jaw still dangled loose, just as it had from the second wave of Veruca's message to her. When the muscle around it finally started working again, all she said was, "Monkey's uncle. Lucien finally found himself a real wizard."

7

After I collected on my bet with Duchess by way of a few strands of her hair, I took her out to breakfast. The victory had taken the sting out of my injury, but by the time I was done eating, pain had crept back in. I thanked Duchess for bringing the items I had asked Valente for and said goodbye. I stopped by Walgreen's to grab a bottle of painkillers, hung the Do Not Disturb sign on my hotel room door, and lay down to take a nap while I waited for the pills to kick in.

No dreams came and by ten-thirty I was as pain-free as I was likely to get. I spent a half-hour straightening up the room, though there was little I could do about the broken mirror. I planned on leaving the Do Not Disturb sign up, but I didn't need an overzealous maid getting me kicked out. Inspecting my work, I thought the room had been upgraded from terrorist aftermath to post-drunken bender.

"*Quit stalling,*" *my inner voice warned.*

"*Yeah, I know. Our real problem is the wendigo. It's just so much easier to deal with the mundane,*" *I admitted.*

"*Magically exploding telephones are mundane?*"

"For this week, yes, yes they are. There hasn't been anything normal about this week. The most "normal" disaster this week was me accidentally bumping Dorothy's light controls out at the lake. I haven't done anything that harebrained since…wait a sec."

"Do I smell an idea?"

"Wild paranoia-slash-conspiracy-theory, but maybe it's an idea: What if I didn't turn Dorothy's headlights on?"

"Umm, you must have. I mean, who else was there? Oh …."

"Starting to see my point?"

"You don't think we ended up in that gas station by accident."

"Nope, it would make a great Murder, She Wrote *plot, but I'm not Jessica Fletcher. A wizard is the first person at the scene of a magical homicide by coincidence? Something wanted me there."*

"So they sabotaged the car. You might be on to something."

"Only one way to find out." I decided. *"We're going back out to the lake."*

8

I n the afternoon sun, it was hot enough that I had to shed not only my jacket, but my t-shirt as well. Only an Oklahoma October could swing so wildly between sweltering during the day and freezing at night. I hung both jacket and shirt over the driver's side mirror to keep them from getting dirty. Now, it was a matter of lying out on Dorothy's hood, soaking up the last warm rays of the year, and waiting. If I was right, I wouldn't have to wait long.

"Nice tattoos," a girl's voice said.

They really are, or at least, I think so. I restricted my body art to places that can't be seen when I'm fully dressed, on the theory that this helps with traffic stops and job interviews. None of them were the result of drinking or peer pressure and most were my own design. I was particularly proud of the chest piece: A Celtic cross with a sun, moon, and stars worked in. Along the arms of the cross was my true name spelled out in characters that were archaic before the Bible was ever written.

I waved at the pair of teenage girls. "Thanks." They continued on their way along the shoreline, but their giggles drifted back to me. Once upon a time, I would have given anything to make young ladies giggle like that. I was always too awkward and gangly when I was of an appropriate age where I could have considered pursuing those two.

True names are a tough magic to appreciate. Reflecting on it, Lucien was very careful not to say his own name out loud in front of me. Likely, he had been told that a wizard could do things if he knew a victim's true name from their own lips. That may be, but most people aren't even aware of their true name. Even if they were, the exact pronunciation required an effort of will. I had even heard of cases where a person's true name changed over time. I was still working on figuring out exactly what mine meant. Part of it derived from the Babylonian for "sworn-sword," while another portion meant "far-wanderer". Taken together, I told people that my tattoo means I was an honorary Knight of the Gypsy Moon. If only there were more than one member, we could have gone on a wendigo-killing crusade together.

"Returning to the scene of the crime, Mr. Fisher?"

I didn't even turn to look. I had half-expected her and was pleased to find that my intuition was not completely broken. "Oh, a crime was committed here, all right. Somebody assassinated my battery. Care to investigate that one, Agent Devereaux?"

"Battery murder? No, that's what happens when you leave your headlights on. I'm more interested in the real murder that took place three miles north of here."

"That? If you've got handcuffs that will fit a wendigo, by all means go arrest it."

"What the hell is a wendigo?" she growled. "Are you withholding …."

I sat upright and spun to face her with fierceness. "Don't play with me, Devereaux. I may not be much of a combat mage, but angry wizards have other ways of expressing their displeasure. Something about 'for thou art crunchy and taste good with ketchup'."

She stood there wearing the same suit I had last seen her in, a blank expression on her face. After a good minute, she said, "I think that's supposed to be about dragons, not wizards."

"Yeah, well, there's some strange stuff going on around here and if I don't start getting some answers, maybe I'll try to summon a dragon tonight. Now…why did you kill my car?"

"How did you figure that out?"

"Your eyes. They're the same color as the lake. They were bugging me the whole interrogation, like a pair of really unnatural contacts. And you kept bringing it back around to the book. Little things, but once I caught up on my sleep, I started doing the math. I hope the real Agent Devereaux isn't hurting too bad."

"No, I just borrowed her for a little bit." She eyed me warily. "What are you …."

I held up my hand to interrupt her. "Nope, you already got to interrogate me once. Now it's my turn, right? Trade for trade, I answered yours, so now you have to answer mine. Or should I call up the faerie queens and kings and tell them you reneged?"

"You wouldn't." Her words said, but her pale expression said she thought I might. "You don't have that kind of juice. They'd eat you alive."

"Maybe I don't. But Lucien Valente does. Should I send out invitations in my boss's name?"

She gulped. I was curious to see what kind of pull his name would have with supernatural creatures not in his employ. I had expected indifference or grudging respect. What I saw in Devereaux's face was fear. "No. You are right. I am in your debt. Will you agree to seven answers?"

"I suspect I gave you more than that…but I will accept seven as a fair trade. I didn't lie to you, so you'll have to be honest with me as well. Those are the terms. Do you agree?"

"Yes, one."

She had me: I did phrase it as a question. "Why did you turn my car's headlights on to bright?"

"I didn't want you to be suspicious about why you had a dead battery. Two."

Her grin made me think thunderous dark thoughts. She was going to run out her debt while giving me as little as possible to work with. "I see. You wanted my battery dead, so that my car wouldn't work, so that I'd have to walk instead of drive. Why did you want me walking that night?"

"Better chance of you meeting someone else. Three."

"Like the wendigo. Did you want us to meet at the gas station when we did, or did you intend for us to end up someplace else?"

"Place was irrelevant. Four."

I ran my right hand through my brown mane, absently pulling a few hairs as I did. "Fine, we'll play it your way. Without adding unnecessary sounds or going outside the range of human hearing, what is the correct pronunciation of your true name?"

Her face instantly filled with panicked, furious thought. "You wouldn't know how to use it."

I reached into my jacket and pulled out my gremlin phone. I twirled it slowly while I stared at her. I said nothing.

"What...what is that?"

"Nope. It's still my turn to ask the questions. You still owe me three answers."

The business suit, no, the skin suit that was Agent Devereaux sloughed off into a puddle at her feet. What was left could have passed as one of the junior high school girls that had walked by...except for her greenish-blue skin and pointed ears. She was clad in a yellow bikini top with white polka dots and a pair of cut-off denim shorts, a major shift from the pressed and starched Agent Devereaux. "Please, Wizard Fisher, don't make me say it."

I crumbled. I had thought I was dealing with a cunning, cold-hearted, arrogant bitch. In retrospect, adolescent snottiness was an equally plausible defense for her attitude.

"Don't care. Adolescent for a lake spirit, even a man-made lake, is still decades older than you," my inner voice advised.

Too late, my heart was already softening. "If I un-ask my last question, will you be more cooperative? I'd really rather be friends than bully you around."

She nodded. "Please un-ask it. I'll do whatever you want."

"Then I un-ask it. And you should be careful about who you give your word to that you will 'do whatever they want.' Some wizards might not feel the same way I do about hurting women and children."

She paled to a slimy, gray color. "Eek...I'm sorry. I've never dealt with a real wizard before. I feel like such a doofus."

I nodded. "It's okay. I'm not all that experienced with the fae myself. You're the first I've met in the flesh...well, and recognized you for what you are."

"I'm a lake spirit. We don't like being called faeries."

"Fair enough. Quick timeout from the formal questions: What should I call you? Agent Devereaux doesn't seem to fit any more."

"No, that's her name. I just borrowed her mind when she came out to see your car."

"And today?"

"Just an illusion...I thought you might be afraid of her."

"So the real Agent Devereaux is..."

"Should be okay, though I doubt she remembers much. Pretty tough brain for a human."

"So back to the real questions: You borrowed her because you wanted to see what your handiwork had accomplished?"

"You could say that, yes. My vision gets kind of fuzzy if I try to go pass the crossroads. I just rode along with her to see what had happened after you left. And you can call me T...ummm, Tia? Yeah, Tia works."

"All right, Tia, I'm Colin." We shook hands again, a very different experience than shaking Devereaux's firm hand. Tia's was soft, delicate, and a little bit slimy. "Explain to me what happened that night."

"I didn't want you staying here. It's not you...I didn't even know you were a wizard then. It's that book."

For half a second, I thought about pretending she meant the Yiddish fairy book, but I knew better than that. "The Necronomicon."

"Yeah. It's bad juju. I tried to convince some of the wood sprites to steal it, but they didn't like all the metal on your car. So I attacked the car myself. I turned the acid in your battery to lake water, then turned on the lights so that you'd think it was by accident. I know all about batteries. Lots of people drain theirs by leaving on the lights or radio on while they...while they, umm ..." Her blush was a deep plum purple, mingled under a navy blue background.

"I understand. Did you mean for me to run into the wendigo?"

"The ice cannibal demon...is that its name?"

"Type, I think. You're a lake spirit; he's a wendigo."

"Okay. Well, I didn't like him any more than I liked the book. So I tried to lead him to the book. I figured they'd kill each other. But the ice demon kept veering off the trail I left for him. When I saw you were both heading the same way, I stopped trying to distract it. Then the police came and I made sure they took the book away with them." She looked nervously towards Dorothy's back seat. "But now it's back again."

I ignored her dislike for the book and stored away for future reference her belief that the book could possibly be a match against a homicidal wendigo. I knew why she didn't care for it.

Heck, I hated the thing myself, but I needed it. The lake spirit had tried to lead the wendigo here, to me, to my book…but the wendigo curse was targeted only at employees of Lucien Valente. The curse must have kept pulling it off the fairy's trail. Once it got loose, it went after the nearest such victim, the drug-dealing gas station attendant. When I interrupted, it wanted to attack me as an interloper. If I hadn't been there, it couldn't touch me: I wasn't a Valente employee back then.

"We are now."

Returning to the immediate problem, I gestured toward the book. "It'll go away soon. I won't bring it back here to your domain again without permission, Lady Tia."

"Thank you, Wizard Colin."

I caught up her hand, took a knee, and lightly brushed my lips across her third knuckle. "No, milady, 'tis my pleasure to honor you. You've been quite helpful today." For what I had in mind now, it wouldn't hurt to lay it on a little thick.

She laughed as I rose, then remembered her manners and curtsied. "I'm sorry I tried to kill you. I was just scared. It's a really bad book."

"You are forgiven, Tia."

"Lady Tia."

"Very well. You are forgiven, Lady Tia." I paused. "Have you ever felt the ice demon's presence before?"

She nodded. "A few times. He always comes from that way." She pointed east by southeast.

A clue. Never mind that twenty percent of the United States stretched out in that general direction. It was a narrower search area than I had previously. "If he came back again, and I was here, could you lead him to me?"

"But, Wizard Colin, he would kill you. I don't want to kill my first wizard friend." She paused. "You are my friend, yes?"

"I would like to be, Lady Tia. And you are right: the wendigo will most likely kill me. But if I were able to face him on the ground of my choosing, with proper preparation…"

Her eyes went wide as she understood. "I think I know just the place. May I show it to you?"

9

"I don't like it," my inner voice warned.

"*What's not to like? If I have to fight a cannibal ice demon, that is. I don't like that part, either.*"

"*The part where the most powerful spellbook we have gets left behind at the hotel room. I know you're feeling your wizardly Wheaties right now, but . . .*"

"*The book stays away. If I bring it back out here, Tia won't help us.*"

"*You've got her wrapped around your little finger. Tell her you need it to slay the demon.*"

"*Weren't you the one telling me how much more ancient and powerful than me she is? I told her it wouldn't come back without her say-so. And I don't want her to be distracted by its presence while she's baiting the wendigo. I can't have my first fairy—sorry, lake spirit princess—getting eaten while she's doing a favor for me.*"

"*Pfui. You'll wish you had it. If the wendigo shows. She's only seen it a few times and it's been active in the area for at least six months.*"

"*I think I can make it show up. But what do you think about Tia's choice of location?*"

"*It'll do. It just might work. That still doesn't mean I like it.*"

The muddy bank she took me to was a triangular wedge, fifteen feet wide by twenty feet deep. Along the wide end, the mud dipped down to the waterline of the lake. The western side was a rocky wall of giant boulders. It was accessible with some trouble, but the path leading up to the boulders was overgrown enough to discourage the effort. The eastern edge of the triangle was a steep dirt slope rising up towards the trees. The combined effect of slope, rock, and water was that this spot very rarely received two-legged visitors. Unlike the rest of the shoreline, I didn't see any discarded bottles, cans, or condoms.

There was a faint buzzing of power in the area, but that could have been the Excedrin wearing off. The mud was dry enough to hold a shape well, promising the possibility of a good magic circle. So long as it wasn't pouring rain, the circle would hold. All I have to do is trap the wendigo inside of it and it would be game, set, point.

"Umm, Colin. If we lure it down here, aren't we trapped too? I mean, unless you know how to fly or can swim faster than a wendigo can?"

"I guess we'll just have to make sure the circle works right the first time around, then."

"Thank you, Lady Tia." I bowed to her. "May I make what preparations I'll need here?"

"You may, Wizard Colin. Shall I see if I can find the ice demon?"

"Not yet. It's Saturday, right?" I did some mental math. "Four nights from now, I think. If I need to change it, I'll let you know. I would not have you say that you did this for me just because I trapped you in a word game. I will pay you for your service, trade for trade."

She shook her head. "Would you buy me like a common girl, wizard? I see much of that along my shores. Is that all you would treat me as? I do not need your payment."

"I told you she was sharper than she looks. Don't let puppy dog eyes fool

you."

"A moment ago you were saying she was wrapped around my pinky."

"No, milady. But valiant heroines deserve a prize when the battle is won."

Her laughter rippled over me in a wave. "Aye. And if the wendigo will talk to you, it is doomed. No demon can possibly outmatch you at the game of tongues."

"I do not plan to talk, but to kill."

Her look was pensive as she stared across the waters of her home. "I wish it were for tongues, Wizard Colin. The ice demon is fierce. Are you sure you will win?"

"No," I confessed. "But I know the odds are better with you on my side. And I must try. I have given my word."

"Very well, Wizard Colin. I shall accept a reward once the creature is dead."

I bowed to her and sat down, Indian style, with my back against the western rock. "And now, adieu, Lady Tia. I must prepare the field."

I blinked for a moment and she was gone. My head was spinning with all things fae. Even the weaker ones, a gremlin and a lake-spirit of a man-made lake, were uncanny with a sense of power the fairy tales couldn't capture. Tia took over the body of an FBI profiler, presumably a strong, disciplined mind, just because she didn't like a book I was carrying. Never mind that she had an intuitive sense of everything that happened near her lake or that she could vanish soundlessly in an instant. If I was this impressed by the low-level pawns, how on Earth was I ever going to serve as an emissary to the fae courts where the big boys and girls played?

"One disaster at a time," the voice said.

"Right you are, though I hate to admit it."

I spent the next hour simply sitting there, my eyes slowly taking in the terrain around me. If I was going to claim home court advantage, I really needed to know the lay of the land: every bump, root, and twig. I took it all in, slowly perfecting my mental picture of the area, changing it with each visual sweep until my psychic model was identical to the physical location.

When I was confident in my mental re-creation, I rose, then sank to one knee, in the position of devotion. I gathered up my energy into the model, rolling the two into a ball the same color as the mud nearest the rock. I moved it up inside of me until it was just below the top of my head, the crown chakra. I took a deep breath and squeezed on the sphere till it burst, the exploding energy filling every nook and cranny of both my sanctuary and me.

"I claim this land as mine. I am your lord and you are my soil, my rocks, my plants, my hill. This is my dominion and I am its master, its steward, its guardian." I paused to let the words roll over and under every leaf, every blade of grass. "Will any dispute my claim? Speak now or forever hold peace."

"None, Lord Wizard," Tia's voice surprised me. I hadn't realized she was still around. "I gift right of this place to you for a year and a day."

Her presence flustered me, even though she supported my claim. The sanctuary ritual was designed to conquer, not receive in gift. I needed her help, though, so I adapted as best I could. "Will any dispute the lady's right to give thee as gift?"

A silent minute passed. The energy I sent out returned to me and with it, a sense of belonging and purpose. This was my land now and both the dirt and I knew it. But what did that mean? I understood the concept of sanctuary, but I had never claimed one before. It was time to experiment and find out. In my mind, I imagined a circle being traced out in the mud in front of me. It took more effort than thought should, but I quickly saw where the extra energy was going. As the psychic circle drew itself out in my head, a matching one appeared in the physical earth at my feet.

I smiled. Wizard one, wendigo zero.

"Technically, it's wendigo six. And what do you think you're going to owe Tia for the gift?"

"Yeah, she ambushed me mid-ritual, the little sneak. I may be her first wizard, but she knew the right time to "gift" me so that I had no choice but to accept it or let the ritual go sour. If she tried it again when I was dealing with the wendigo, it could get me killed."

"I wouldn't worry about that."

"Why not?" I wondered.

"If you're dead, how is she going to collect her reward? Or the debt you now owe for the gifted land?"

"So, do we go with it?"

"Better here than elsewhere. But how are you going to get the wendigo to come to the lake?"

"The curse is targeting Valente employees, right? And it gets stronger by eating its victims," I told the voice.

"With you so far ...."

"Tuesday night is the start of the full moon. Anything it's doing to grow itself will be far more effective then. It'll want a snack or three."

"But it attacked twice this week. What makes you think it will wait that long?"

"Tia set it up one of the times. Maybe the last wizard was out hunting for it before the other attack and it was self-defense rather than hunger. Barring that, I don't know. I just think it will wait."

"Okay, but there's got to be hundreds of Valente employees in the state. Subsidiaries of subsidiaries of subsidiaries, remember? Why is it going to come after us?"

"Who said it would?"

I picked up my grem-phone, pressed zero, and asked for Duchess Deluce. There were no birds in the background while I waited, but an echoing water drip made me think of a vast underground cavern.

"Valente International." The irritation in her voice amused me. There was just something about bothering people that weren't used to being toyed with that made it that much more fun.

"So what does the caller ID read?"

"Fisher?" She growled. "Rubbing in your victory?"

"Nah, I'm over it. Look, I'm calling about the whole curse thing."

"Giving up already?"

"Nope. I think I've got it under control. I just need one little thing…can you throw together a company picnic? Say, all Valente employees in Oklahoma City and Tulsa, northwest parking lot of Lake Thunderbird State Park, Tuesday night, starting at six PM and running till midnight?"

There was a brief pause as I waited for her to explain to me why it was logistically impossible. Instead, her response was, "Are we serving hamburgers or hot links?"

10

I was getting worn thin, so I did what any good wizard would do: I had fun. Magic is will and belief. That's a fancy way of saying that it comes from inside you. As a Catholic, I believe it's part of what it means to be made in the image of God: everything He can do, I can, too, just on a smaller scale. Of course, He's got several billion years of experience on me and presumably limitless energy resources, whereas I am fully enclosed within the laws of thermodynamics. So if I was going to go around flinging magic out of me, I needed to do something to bring energy back into me.

The first shopping center I stopped at didn't appeal to me. Dorothy and I hadn't been spending as many miles together as usual, so I found another mall clear across town on the map. I took a roundabout way and might have kept my foot a little heavier on the gas pedal than was ideal, but a guy has to show his car he loves her somehow. The next mall had me hooked the instant I saw the store directory: a Ghiradelli chocolatiers and a video arcade. Energy intake didn't get any better than good chocolate and pinball.

My stop at Ghiradelli required little in the way of explanation. My purchases fell into three categories: chocolate I ate while still in the store, chocolate I ate while still in the mall, and chocolate I would eat later on. I bought enough to feed a platoon for several days, that is to say, enough to last me 'til Tuesday. Maybe. I justified the extravagance by telling myself I might have to trade some of it to a hungry fairy.

"Hey, no need for that. If your soul is on the market, I can get us a great deal on some heavy hitters from the outer darkness. The wendigo won't know what hit him."

"Neither my chocolate, nor my soul, is going anywhere," I assured my inner voice.

"Oh, come on. Have you ever seen it? Touched it? You'll barely even miss…hey, put that down…mmph mmrrm."

"That's better."

After Ghiradelli, I had to stop by the ATM. I wasn't out of pocket change yet, but based on my last few shopping experiences since meeting Valente, I would be broke by the time I left the mall. Nothing from the nefarious electronic spaces tried to eat me or my debit card while I used the machine. From there, I went around in a whirlwind of capitalism. I got a new pair of jeans, some new steel-toed boots, a couple of CDs (yes, people still buy those, Internet problems, remember?), a leather duffel bag, titanium-rimmed sunglasses, and a katana. I had no delusions about the quality of the sword, but I was so surprised to see one for sale in a mall that I bought it on general principle. Against some spirits, especially the fae, any steel is better than no steel.

"Rrhhrrm mmrph."

"Yeah, I know. Karmic balance means that against some spirits, steel, regardless of quality, will be worthless. Given my luck, wendigoes will probably fall into that category. Now, shut up, and let me enjoy my last Saturday on planet Earth."

The arcade was everything I hoped for. There was a prize counter for trading in tickets earned in the skill games, tons of older machines, and a few of those new-fangled work-out-while-you-play type games. Looking over the prize case, my eye settled on one of the bins and I decided it was time for a little skee-ball. My hand-eye coordination wasn't what it used be in my Xbox in the dorm room days, but I figured the game out soon enough. I blew through five bucks worth of tokens, racking up what I needed for the item in the case, and had a blast doing it.

After that, I wandered through the aisles, stopping to play anything that looked even remotely fun: a new Street Fighter, old school Space Invaders, some game with a winged chimp, an alien shoot-em-up game that mixed in cowboys and dinosaurs. I dropped coins in all of them. The pinball selection was not up to my exacting standards, but I played each machine once just to make sure. I was in a generous mood and started leaving an extra token or two on top of each machine when I was done. What good was a dangerous job with a huge paycheck if I couldn't spend it all?

I had gotten my inner groove back.

11

I forced myself to enjoy a sit down meal at a restaurant that didn't specialize in early bird specials. I debated a glass of wine, but felt guilty knowing I'd be driving Dorothy afterward. I wasn't a wine guy, anyway. I hoped Lucien Valente didn't expect his personal wizard to attend his social parties. I was not much for beer, either, but I doubted that was an issue in his circles.

After dinner, I drove back to the hotel, dropped off the Necronomicon, half the remaining chocolates, my old boots, and a few things I didn't think I'd be needing. On a whim, I picked up the hairs I had taken from Duchess after winning the magical phone bet, then headed back to the lake.

Once I was back behind Dorothy's wheel, I released the gag from my darker half.

"Zₓₓₓ."

He pretended to be asleep, his idea of revenge for being silenced for so long. I could have used some advice, because there was a possibility that what I had planned was suicidally stupid.

"Zₓₓₓ. Zₓₓₓ."

I was pretty sure he would wake up if my life were at risk. The fact that he was still pretending to snooze was my green light. If everything went south, I could blame my subconscious for not telling me to stop.

I took out my prizes from the arcade and my leftover tickets. When I finished writing on the tickets, I folded them up, put them where I wanted them, and inspected my work. In low light, the surface of the beads glittered, but the tickets were nearly invisible. I was satisfied they would accomplish what I needed them to do.

From the hotel, it was a thirty-minute drive to Lake Thunderbird. I had made it in less than that earlier, but after dark the road was treacherous. I decided I didn't like these woods at night whether I was on foot or nestled away behind Dorothy's steel shell. Bad things had happened here. I suspected that was part of what the wendigo liked about them.

The sign out front said the park was closed, but no physical barriers blocked my progress. I selected a parking spot not easily seen from the main road. I doubted my presence here could amount to anything more serious than a misdemeanor, but I didn't want to direct unnecessary legal attention my way. The FBI still thought I might be a serial killer in the making and one of their agents might be grumpy post-fae possession.

I gathered up everything I would need for the ritual into my new duffel bag, along with a few items I wouldn't. It never hurts to be over-prepared. I headed out into the midnight shadows of the forest, grateful for what moonlight there was. Closer to the lake, the woods weren't quite so scary, but I still had quite an adventure getting out there. If I hadn't been able to hone in on *my* land instinctively, I'm not sure I would have found it. Privacy was part of its attraction, but tough for others to access also meant tough for me to access. It was a necessary evil: I was going to need my sanctuary for what I was about to try.

Once I got there, I set out my prizes from the arcade first, placing each just inside the watery edge of my domain, making sure the lighting was just right. They were within a hair of the waterline, but they were still on my side and that was what counted. With that trap set, I proceeded to the preparations for the night's real work. Using the tip of my staff, I carefully drew out a five foot circle, simultaneously syncing it up with my mental representation of the space. Once I was satisfied with it, I pulled my ritual dagger (athame in magic lingo) and carefully carved out the internal markings I would need for a summoning.

The near-disaster with the gremlin had produced some interesting results and boosted my confidence as a summoner. Magic that didn't kill me made me smarter. But a magical cellphone, as cool as it was, wasn't what I had been looking for. I wanted a face-to-face talk with a faerie. I needed a spirit guide, someone who could explain wendigoes and spirit wars to me in terms I was familiar with.

I had placed all the candles, seventeen in total tonight, and was lighting a stick of incense I had set into the western rock face when my first guest arrived. I felt her fingers, moist but warm, slide down on to my shoulders. I let her rub my back, enjoying the sensation. "I was wondering if you were going to show up, Tia."

"Lady Tia, remember?" Her voice was husky with evening shadow.

I glanced up to see her face behind me. She was young and pretty, thought the aqua green skin would take some getting used to, even at night. She had traded in her bikini top for a more sensible sweatshirt. A trio of mardi gras beads in purple, silver, and gold hung from her neck. "My land, my rules. I am the lord here." She pouted, so I continued, "But hospitality is important, so I shall call you milady if it pleases you."

"It does, Lord Wizard Colin. What brings you back out here

this night? Is all of this just to see me?"

"I have work to do, milady. And I was eager for you to receive your gift." I gestured toward the beaded necklaces.

"A gift? No, I found these unattended."

"On my land, not yours."

A deep frown sank into her lips. "Perhaps you are mistaken. Perchance you brought me similar gifts and I may have found these elsewhere."

I nodded thoughtfully. "It is possible. But mine had tags on them." I pulled one of the prize tickets from my pocket. "They are marks of the fierce battle in the electric dungeon that I had to endure to win milady her gift."

She twisted the necklaces around, revealing to her dismay the folded up tickets I had wrapped around each string. She pulled one off and examined it, reading out loud, "Captain Hook's Funland."

"Read the other side," I suggested.

She flipped it over. "To Lady Tia, From Colin Fisher." Her breath came out in a hiss that sounded like water being forced through a rusted pipe. The she slumped. "A gift, then."

"Shall we call it splits, milady? A gift for a gift, the land for the beads?" I put an edge to my voice before I finished. "Or are you determined to try to trump the wizard again?"

"A gift for a gift. I'll behave." She stared out across the lake. "It's not like I was going to make you do anything too nasty to square it. I just wanted to tell people that I had a wizard indebted to me. That's a pretty big deal."

"Oh?" I was curious what a lake spirit's idea of not too nasty was. "And when the time came to collect, what were you going to suggest?"

"You know, the usual. Give me a human child to raise or get me with child, whatever. Or there's some boys who keep spitting tobacco juice into me when they're fishing; you could turn them into worms or something." She paused. "You know, I could always find another gift for you if any of those options sound appealing. You wouldn't have to do it right away, you know, let me have a couple years to brag first."

I didn't want to know what sort of repayment Tia thought of as nasty.

12

O nce Tia and I came to an understanding on magical etiquette (most notably with instructions that she was not to offer me unasked-for gifts in the middle of rituals on my land), she yawned and said she was getting sleepy. I suspected she was disappointed about me getting the drop on her and just wanted a little privacy to sulk. I nodded and told her that was fine, I could handle the ritual from here. She left, but I was pretty sure she was still paying attention to what I was doing. I wondered just how much awareness a lake spirit had regarding the area around her lake. Did she see the whole thing at once or was it a matter of where she was focused at a given moment?

I eventually ignored the question and returned to my original task. With candles lit, lines drawn, and incense burning, all that was left was to arrange the seven flawlessly white hairs Duchess had given me after the Veruca Wakefield bet. I laid one along each grooved line of the paired triangles. The seventh I wrapped around a chocolate square and placed it dead center of the circle. Using the chocolate hurt, but it was one little square and I knew where the store was if I ran out. I was tempted to add a drop of my own blood, but I resisted. I needed the ritual to work, and I wasn't an experienced enough summoner to know how the blood magic would interact with it. A line from a nightmare flickered across my mind in Sarai's dream voice: *Blood of a virgin, better be careful.*

While genuflecting, I pulled in my energy slower than usual— I had been too quick on the draw with the gremlin, not cautious and controlled enough. On top of that, I was working with a lot more energy tonight. I had topped off my tank at the mall, true, but there's a big difference between a hotel room and a lakeside sanctuary. The background energy at the hotel was low and stale, something to be suppressed or ignored while casting. Here, natural currents of wild energy flowed from plant to plant, a steady trickle descending down to the water's edge. As I gathered in my own aura, my new sanctuary eagerly rushed in to fill the void. It was cool, exciting, and forbidden, like skinny-dipping on a summer night.

As I tried to center it all into the focused sphere, I realized there was more available to me here than I could ever possibly hold. I breathed out, then tried to pull in a little bit more energy with the next inhale. Repeating it over ten breaths, I amassed a solid softball-sized chunk of will and power inside of me. I let the rest of the sanctuary's aura wash over me, wrapping it around myself like a cloak, while I held the spell steady. When I was certain I could control what I had gathered, I let the ball hover around my solar plexus, the center of my strength. It had to be an improvement over the voice-centered gremlin calling spell.

After the buildup, the magic itself was fast and simple. "Flesh calls to flesh, spirit to spirit. Unseelie ancestor, answer my summons." Releasing the energy stored in my chest required little more than flexing.

I felt the energy fly, but the results were not spectacular. The hairs and the chocolate dissolved slowly, as if corroded by an invisible acid. I waited, still on one knee, but nothing else happened. My host of candles flickered, burned lower, but none gutted out. No explosions, no flying shrapnel, nothing. Disappointment at the return to my usual low standards of magic began to set in.

It wasn't until I actually looked at one of the candles that I realized my initial assessment was seriously flawed. The flame was as tall as it had been, but the color and brightness were draining away. Where it should have been blue and orange, it was now a greasy purple and gray. I reached out with my left hand and found the heat was fading as well, making the flame barely warmer than the surrounding air, though the wax still melted freely. I forced my will into the candles through my internal sanctuary and the wicks burst back to a vibrant orange. In response, the breeze carried a soft hiss to my ear; its touch was cold and sharp.

I closed my eyes and shifted my attention to the mental representation of the sanctuary again, focusing on the direction the sound had come from. On the very edge of my land, where rock and slope came together at the inland point of the wedge, there was a shape that was more shadow than substance. As the candlelight died down to a dim mockery of its true self again, the form relaxed and became fuller, more humanoid. I shivered partially from the dropping temperature, partially from the sense of power emanating out from the visitor.

"Thank you for coming," I intoned.

My guest was gaunt, its black, billowing robes shifting so freely in the wind that I entertained the possibility that nothing physical, corporeal, lay underneath. The cowl on top tilted slightly when I spoke, as if considering me. A pale gray hand slipped from the cavernous folds and slowly brushed back the hood. White hair the color of bleached bone slipped free, framing a face as beautiful as it was terrible. The outline held the ideal lines of the feminine form, only slimmer, unnaturally narrow. Her lips were plump and full, but black as slick tar. The rest of her face was gray like her hand, save where the hollow of her eyes receded. So deep were the shadows around them, I was not entirely certain she had eyes at all.

"You can see me." At least, I thought that was what she said. Her voice was a low whisper, cracked as if from severe disuse.

I spoke softly in answer. She looked so fragile, I feared a loud noise might break her. "I can. You are Duchess' blood?"

"You used my granddaughter to call me? You are either very powerful or very reckless, wizard. The Eye of Winter is not lightly paged." I had to calm my heartbeat. I could barely hear her over the sound of my blood pumping, but she seemed to sense this, speaking only between beats.

"I am ...." She held up a skeletally thin hand to silence me.

"The Eye of Winter sees who you are, Colin Fisher. And what you want. Trade is trade. What do you offer for the knowledge you seek?"

I was dreading this part. The least slip of my tongue could bind me to a hundred years of slave labor or worse. "If you know what I desire, you know what a fair price is. Tell me the cost and I will tell you whether I am willing to pay it."

"Life." Only that word and nothing more.

"Whose life? What life?"

"Not yours and not by your hand. One life is the price."

"To learn about wendigoes and spirit wars I must become a murderer?"

"No." I heard amusement in her whispered reply. "A life is what it will cost to know of Sarai."

"Sarai?" My answer was louder than I intended and she flinched at the sound.

"You asked the fair price for what you desired. The Eye of Winter has told you."

A life? For Sarai, no, for knowledge of Sarai? The longer I lingered with that temptation the more trouble I would be in. "What of the wendigo?"

"Fear not, wizard-knight, my offer will stand when you are ready. One life for what you desire to know." A smile curved over her lips. "For the wendigo, I will only ask another piece of chocolate."

I quickly dug one out of the bag. She floated toward me and knelt down across from me. When she licked the chocolate square from my fingers, our brows were nearly touching, but I still couldn't see her eyes. It seemed as if her sockets receded back into darkness forever. I wondered if she had any eyes at all or, if not, what horrors dwelled in those holes instead. "Why so cheap?"

"It is good chocolate," she confessed. "And you must know that my prices are fair. There could be much business between us, Colin Fisher. Long has it been since so intriguing a mortal has willingly called me up." She paused. "Ask."

"What is the wendigo?"

"A spirit of hunger. In the time before time, faceless men taught the winter wolf to eat both flesh and soul. It has never known a full belly since."

"Faceless men?" Where had I heard that phrase before? A different voice had spoken of them and the phrase echoed around inside me as if I knew the answer.

"They are not relevant to now. You are not ready for that knowledge, Colin Fisher."

Her breath nearly gagged me when she spoke my name. It was full of warm spice overlaying cold decay. When I had recovered, I said, "And the spirit wars forced the wendigo to slumber. How?"

"Once, all sons of Adam and daughters of Eve were one race, one people. But after they were broken, their strength was not what it once had been."

"The tower of Babel?"

"It is one story: Babel, Atlantis, Avalon, Pangaea. Many tales, one truth. The survivors who fled to this land found many enemies waiting for them. Arrogant spirits thought man's dominion had ended. Mad spirits driven insane by the faceless set upon them. Without the strength of unity, the humans were easy prey for the monsters around them. Millennia after the falling time, the remnants of your people were still in fear of these beasts.

"The stories most commonly speak of twins who ventured beyond the edge of the world to bring back salvation. When they returned, they brought the spirit war. The tribes swore allegiance to the twins until all the people of this land were one people. Spirits of summer and spirits of crafting were appeased with offerings and promises and lent their strength to the twins' army."

"Offerings?" I asked.

"Do not play ignorant, knight-wizard. You know what the sun gods demanded for their aid. Winter is not the only thing that hungers for mortal life. Do not confuse our quarrel with the Seelie as a matter of good versus evil." Visions of people lying on stone altars atop block pyramids, waiting for the dagger to fall, danced through my mind.

"I will remember, Eye of Winter. Please continue."

"Their full strength rode to the Shadowlands, determined to purge the world of monsters like the wendigo. One-fifth came back from that dark place, carrying the peace of the twins. The dark spirits would slumber and men would not walk in the Lands of Shadow. This peace has held for all of written history."

"How did the curse wake it?"

"No," she whispered firmly.

"No?"

"The curse did not wake it. It only strengthened it, reminded the wendigo of the path from the Shadowlands to this realm. It was already awake."

"Why? Why is it waking?"

"Some can be reached in their dreams. If people turn to cannibalism, the wendigo dreams it. From there, it might hunt in its sleep, but it will return to its hibernation."

"Cannibalism," I said.

"Not this one. Someone is walking the Shadowlands. Their footsteps echo in the night. The peace of the twins is broken and soon all the sleeping spirits will rise."

"Armageddon." Verses of Revelation came unbidden out of my memory.

"Apocalypse," she corrected. "Armageddon is a battle to end all battles. This will be a one-sided slaughter."

"So the person who wrote the curse is traveling through the Shadowlands waking things up?"

"No," she whispered.

"No?"

"The person who cursed Valente is not strong enough to walk the Shadowlands. The two events are not directly related."

"Not directly. But there is a link?"

"There are many links, Colin Fisher. For example, you tie both events together by your interest."

I needed the right question, but I couldn't come up with it. The Eye of Winter was trying to avoid saying something and I suspected she had centuries of experience at not saying things she didn't want to say. I would need to offer a greater payment or be satisfied with what she was willing to give. "Tell me what you want to tell me."

"There is much that I want to tell you, Colin Fisher. Perhaps I will have the chance if you focus on the immediate. Kill the wendigo and break the curse. Overreach too soon, too fast, and you will die."

I nodded. She made sense. The wendigo was enough without worrying about faceless men or a shadow-walker. "How do I kill it?"

"The peace is broken, but the twins' allies are still bane to their enemies."

"Summer and steel," I said.

"Use what belongs to them and you can hurt it." She paused. "Or let winter flow through your veins and you can control it, turn it back against your foes." Her fingers reached up and slowly dragged along my cheek. "I could show you how, wizard-knight."

The air grew colder almost instantly. My skin rose in goose bumps in response to the heady mix of chill, thrill, and terror. "I cannot pay the price for such a gift, Eye of Winter."

Her smile was filled with pity and premonition. "The day is coming when you will wish that you had. But the choice that is made cannot be unmade." She leaned forward and the stench of her breath grew thick around me. "But you have not answered me as to the girl. When you are ready to know of Sarai, you need only speak my name and I will come."

What she whispered in my ear next, her lips almost pressed to my frozen lobe, was so terrible, so crushingly sad, so unspeakable, I forgot each word as soon as the sound passed. Only the emotion remained, the horrific certainty that what remained of my life was so disturbing, so violated, that when death finally found me, I would be grateful.

Days passed as we knelt there in the cold and stink. "What did you say?"

The Eye of Winter leaned back and smiled. "I told you your true love's story."

13

T he fairy was gone, but her taint remained, like a frozen fetid blanket over my sanctuary. I tried to help the natural currents of energy wash away her lingering presence, but I was too distracted to be of much help. The Eye of Winter was high fae. She couldn't outright lie. If she said that she had whispered the story of my true love to me, then she had. She might have mixed in other things as well, but then she might not have. I didn't think she had. She had told me about my love life, past, present, and future, and it had two effects on me. First, the defense mechanisms in my brain were valiantly trying to wipe every memory of every syllable from my synapses. The second reaction was to tear me between killing myself or making those responsible for such tragedy suffer horrific torments.

"Given your past loves, suicide and revenge probably amount to the same thing."

"There you are, I was starting to hope you were gone."

"You wish. I just didn't like playing around with the Oracle of the Unseelie Court."

"You could have warned me," I pointed out.

"I didn't know who Duchess was related to until after. And...wait a sec, where's the Necronomicon?"

"The hotel, remember?"

"Why am I awake then? I wasn't going to wake up, unless...oh shit."

"What?"

"Colin, how long has it been this cold?"

"The Eye of Winter brought it with her."

"Are you sure?"

I sniffed at the air. The foul sewage smell of her breath was almost gone. A glance at the half-burned candles showed they were back to a normal orange flame. But the cold was still as strong as when she was...I jumped to my feet, grabbing my athame and the nearest candle.

What happened next was a frantic blur, more reaction that thought. Even as I rose, a whitish gray mass like a giant snowball crashed down from the top of the rock. I flailed an arm, backpedaling. Something solid, cold, hit my forearm. The dagger ripped out of my grip. The whirling mass of snow and fur yelped and spun. My brain suggested teeth like sharp icicles were lunging at me, but the foe was as formless as a blizzard. I swung hard with my other arm.

Candle and hot wax collided with something. Fire sizzled out on contact. The wendigo screamed, a howling storm wind. It sprinted away, trying to escape. It should have kept coming. My weapons were gone, but the fire must have scared it. I tapped into my mental sanctuary. With a thought, weeds and branches on the upslope lashed together, blocking its flight.

Frustrated, it turned back to fight. This was my game now; its surprise advantage was spent. Three candles sat between me and its charge path. I shoved all the energy I could into tiny flames, willing them to life. I couldn't throw a fireball, but amping up existing fire was different. The triplet of candles belched out a curtain of fire. The wendigo's momentum hurdled it through the blast. What came out on the other side looked more hairless Saint Bernard than ice demon. Without its veil of winter, it was reduced to an oversize dog. I softened the mud under its paws, sinking it up to its belly. Its body temperature quickly froze the ground into a prison.

While it struggled, I ran to my duffel bag. I had to finish this now. An ancient evil might underestimate me once, but if it escaped, it would never enter the sanctuary again, no matter how well baited. I snatched out the mall-bought katana, yanked it from its sheath, and charged. I stabbed with it, silly me, and for one dread moment, I thought the sword would snap in two. But steel was steel and, under my weight, it plunged into the wendigo's flesh halfway to the hilt. The wendigo yelped, then sank prone. Its black blood poured out on the ground in a sheet.

I collapsed to the ground. My left arm was numb, half-frozen from where the wendigo had landed on me. My right shoulder was complaining about the sword thrust and I suspected its complaints would only get louder. But my heart was still connected to the rest of my body and the wendigo was dead.

"Are you sure?"

I started to object, but I had seen my fair share of horror movies.

I groped around for my dagger, but didn't find it. I grabbed my staff instead and forced myself back to my feet. I smashed the wood against its head. When I tried to lift it for a second swing, my shoulder firmly declared that was enough of that. My legs were relatively fine, so I gave it a solid kick. The third such steel-toe kiss knocked the beast free of the frozen Earth. With its belly exposed, I solved one of the mysteries of the evening: The hilt of my vanished athame barely poked out from its chest. I understood then why it had been so eager to retreat: its initial pounce had impaled it. Sometimes it's better to be lucky than good.

THIRD INTERLUDE

The hulking giant knelt deeply before his mistress, his feathery wings spread prostrate at Lilith's feet. "The vampire is clever for one of his lineage. He is steadily resisting the temptations and …."

Uriel's deep tone was interrupted by a loud popping noise, followed by a frantic high-pitched squeaking disguised as a voice. "My lady, my lady, I bring terrible news."

Uriel growled, the death angel's words laced with violence. "I was granted audience, imp."

Lilith lifted one foot and pressed her spiked heel deep into Uriel's muscular shoulder. "And the audience bores me already. You have your orders concerning Dr. Green. I suggest you follow them." She turned her attention to the imp, her ember red eyes drilling through him. "Do not bore me, imp."

The creature was more shadow than substance, giant oversize wings and long, lithe tail concealing the tiny devil-body connecting them. "An Atlantean, my lady."

"There are many Atlanteans, foul slave. As I recall, there were seventeen million of them when their empire fell."

The imp stuttered. "No, no…a knight, my lady. One of their knights is back."

Lilith smiled, a thing of sensuous beauty, though all in the chamber realized how much more dangerous it made her look. "I know this. One of my best chaos demons escorts him even now. He is already pact-bound to us."

"Not Darien, my lady. Another has come." The imp trembled, desperately not wanting to be here. He was used to scaring, not being scared. His hissing voice was a near inaudible squeak. "The lord knight."

Uriel interjected, "The Lords of Atlantis are gone, never to return. The Faceless Men did their job well on that count."

Lilith ground her heel further in, a narrow crimson line now flowing from Uriel's shoulder. "Hush, angel." She paused. "The lord knight was a knight, not a true lord. He has been back many times. He is always too obsessed with his petty vendettas and his nymph to be of any real threat. It is that way with old souls. Fifty thousand years of mortal passions tends to render them distracted and useless."

The imp paused, wishing it could have tricked someone else into delivering this message. "He has been brought into the game."

That rattled the Queen of the Nine Hells. "What?" Her eyes narrowed dangerously. "He has made a pact?"

"Not with us."

Uriel roared with what must have passed as laughter in the mouth of a merciless killer. "Heaven would not take an Atlantean."

Lilith flexed her leg again, silencing him. "No, no, they wouldn't. Now quit talking and just look pretty, muscle-boy." Her eyelids fluttered shut, then back open. "You are sure it is the lord knight?"

The imp nodded, then remembered it was hiding its head

between its massive bat wings. "Yes, my lady. He has made a blood pact with Yog …."

"SILENCE!" Lilith screamed, cutting him off. "Do not speak that name here!"

The imp coughed. "But how do you know who I speak of?"

"There is only one entity the lord knight of Atlantis would find common cause with." She removed her stiletto from the death angel's shoulder. "My husband must be told."

No sooner was it thought than the dark lady, the imp, and the fallen archangel were in the grand hall of Asmodeus himself. When Lilith leaned over to whisper in her estranged husband's ear, the assembled devils, demons, and forgotten gods of that gathering saw something not seen since a young Jewish carpenter had entered that very chamber, post-mortem, two thousand years ago. Asmodeus, King of All Hell, Emperor of Himself, Lord of the Abyssal Horde, and Rightful Owner of All Souls, visibly paled.

When he spoke, it was not to anyone in particular, as if he was reminiscing in private rather than seated on his throne before his subjects. "The bastard finally did it. Good for him."

He turned to his lieutenant. "Bar the gates and triple the guard. I doubt it will stop him, but I'd like a few minutes' warning before he walks in on us."

Turning back towards Lilith, "The party is about to get started, my dear. Got another war left in you?"

The beautiful demoness, first wife to Adam, said nothing, only smiled. On the inside, she wondered if this would finally be the conflict that let her slip the dagger into her husband's back.

PART FOUR

THE FEMALE OF THE SPECIES

"You know the difference between Hell's fury and a scorned woman? If you keep your wits about you, you might have a chance of surviving Hell in one piece."

1

I was pretty full of myself as I made my way back to Dorothy. Not only had I cashed the biggest paycheck I'd ever seen, I'd actually earned it. The wendigo was dead. I had his severed head in my duffel bag to prove it. I am wizard, hear me roar. Never mind that I could barely walk straight or that my shoulder was dislocated. As I strolled out of the woods, I felt like a god.

The wind was knocked out of my bloated air bag when I got back to the parking lot. In the back of my head, I was worried about a park ranger ticketing Dorothy. The idea of cops or a tow truck showing up at this time of night was outlandish, but possible. But what I saw there had not even occurred to me as a remote outside chance.

Dorothy had been murdered. No other word came close to describing what had transpired. All four tires were not just flat, but shredded. The windows were covered in sheets of ice; the front windshield had collapsed under the weight. The rear driver's side door had been torn off the hinges. Deep sets of four parallel lines gouged the metal in a helter-skelter fashion, looking like the claw marks of a dog digging in wet mud. Dorothy's hood and trunk were crumpled like discarded paper and tossed several yards away from her corpse. Both bore a crescent ring of small holes that reminded me of a very large dental impression. The engine was a tangle of torn wires and hoses; it didn't take a mechanical genius to see that not all of the parts were there anymore. Her heart, or the engineering equivalent, had been ripped out. Car-cide, plain and simple.

I circled the damage five or six times, trying to convince myself there was some hope of salvage. There wasn't, not even if I summoned a horde of gremlins.

As the shock faded, anger rose to replace it. I wanted to resurrect the wendigo just so I could kill it again, very, very slowly. Failing that, I ….

"Hey, Colin? I appreciate the sudden surge of homicidal intent, but …."

"But what?"

"Not all those claw marks look the same size. And those bite marks…its mouth didn't look nearly that large."

I walked towards the front end, avoiding the dark puddles of gasoline, oil, and anti-freeze as best I could. I didn't have to look hard to confirm my fears. The marks appeared in three different widths—medium, large, and not-quite-Godzilla size. If there had been only two sets, I might have tried to justify it as the difference between front and rear claws. But three …. I held up my hand for comparison to each grouping. I was fairly certain the one I killed had claws close to the large set, but well below the giant set.

I stumbled backward and crashed down on my butt. My balance was usually pretty good, but this was more than I could handle as rage mingled with fright. There were two more wendigoes out there, at least. One of them had claws that spanned well wider than the one I had barely, luckily, managed to kill. I didn't know much about canine paw-to-body size ratio, but

I suspected that meant at least another fifty to a hundred pounds of total body weight. Looking at the way the Detroit steel had been shredded, I decided most of that extra mass was muscle.

Why had only one attacked me? If all of them had worked as a pack, I would have been dead meat, sanctuary or no sanctuary. The one I killed must have found me first, but why didn't the others pounce while I was finishing him off? I turned my attention to the smallest indentations. They were shallow, more insult than injury. If the biggest one was a hundred pounds heavier, the smallest could be fifty pounds lighter, barely more than a large puppy.

I processed the facts and found them unpleasant but satisfactory: the increased rate of attacks, the supernatural heavyweight scared off by a half-assed shield spell, the varying claw sizes. I didn't like it, but they added up. The smaller marks belonged to a baby, a newborn wendigo out on its first hunt with mom and dad. The wendigoes ....

"God, how I hate that plural."

The wendigoes had been feeding more often to support the pregnant mother. When she ran from me at the store, it wasn't because my magic was a threat to her...but it might have been a danger to the thing in her womb.

So what had I killed? It was male, a fact I had learned while digging my dagger free from its belly. Typically, in Earth nature, males are physically larger than the females. But I didn't know if that applied to Shadowlands biology. Still, I leaned towards father rather than an older child. Baby or no, a mother would have rushed in at me to avenge her child's death. But a father might be expendable. She wouldn't want to risk her newborn to fight me in my sanctuary.

"Of course, we aren't in the sanctuary right now."

That got me back on my feet and moving. I loaded up what I could out of Dorothy's remains, though a lot of my library was little more than papier-mâché now. I had unpacked some things into the hotel room earlier, but I was still going to have to leave a lot behind. Not wanting the cops to find my vehicle here, mauled and half-frozen, I removed her identifying marks. The license plate had been torn off and partially shredded, but the VIN number on the dash required a little effort with my Swiss army knife.

There was enough gasoline pooled around her for a funeral pyre, but my lighter was gone. I fumbled around in my pockets.

"This is taking too long, Colin."

"Yeah, I know. She could be back any second. She's probably taking the baby back to the den and then coming for me with a vengeance."

Looking at the ruins of my Dorothy, that sounded all right; millennia-old nursing mother or not, the bitch was going to pay for this.

"Not if we die first. Here, let me speed this up."

I felt my right hand wave, watched it happen more as a spectator than an actor. A surge of power went out through my palm. The puddles under the car began to spit out black smoke as pale green flames appeared at the edges. The energy expenditure made me feel dizzy, light-headed, but I was still aware of the growing heat as the flames rapidly spread.

"Can't pass out on me yet. We've got to get out of here."

I had a vague sensation of walking, stumbling, as my battered body moved away from Dorothy's pyre. Then the pain and exhaustion caught up with me and everything went black.

2

I won't detail my escape from the park last night, largely because I couldn't remember it. I assumed it was long, but uneventful, because it was nearly noon by the time I woke up in my hotel room. Going to Mass was out, but at least I was alive and in one piece. My head throbbed dully, but I didn't feel any unexpected bumps or bruises. In fact, given my certainty that I had dislocated a shoulder last night, I felt pretty damn good. My left arm was slightly tender from where the wendigo landed on my dagger, but I had most of my mobility and the pain was not full-blown frostbite. A couple of Excedrin down the hatch might be enough to get me up and running at full speed.

Waking up went faster after I saw what was on the pillow next to me. The black leather of the Necronomicon was open, its yellowed folio pages casually settled to a page that was mercifully free of illustrations or sketches. I quickly checked behind every door and inside every piece of furniture, then checked them all again before I was satisfied I was alone in the room. I tried to ignore the writing on the open pages, but couldn't help seeing the title of the essay on "Manipulating the Color and Shape of Space and Time" etched at the top. I closed the book and stuffed it in the bottom dresser drawer, opposite a well-worn Gideon's Bible. It was not the first time that memory loss and that damnable tome had been paired. The aftermath of previous occurrences made this one all the more frightening.

I shoveled back a handful of Excedrin, far more than what was strictly necessary for my minor league headache. I wanted to partake in the holy sacraments more than ever, but it was too late in the day for a morning Mass. I considered finding a phone book to see if I could come up with an evening service. Beyond that, the day was a blank slate. I doubted many stores or public buildings would be open on Sunday this deep in the Bible belt. People were probably still at church for a potluck supper or at home watching football. October is still football season, right?

The idea of "at home" caught in my head as my eyes landed on the packet of stuff I had requested from Lucien. There was one person in this state I wanted to be at home today, though I doubted she was much of a churchgoing, pigskin fan. Sitting around trying not to think about what I was doing with the Necronomicon last night was not likely to be productive, but finding her would do wonders for my sense of security. I grabbed the pendant necklace I had bought at Gaea's Treasures and the woman's letter to Valente and got busy. Object reading wasn't my specialty, but I had a luck-based tracking spell that was fairly decent. A severed wendigo head might convince her that she was in over her head and that it was time to call off the curse.

I doubted it though. From the angry, hateful, caustic tone of her letter, I doubted she cared. She wanted Lucien to suffer and didn't really care if she had to die for that to happen. I just hoped I wouldn't have to oblige her. Killing a cannibal ice demon was one thing; killing a woman, even a demented, insane one who riled up ancient demons, was another thing entirely. But even if she did call it off Valente International…the wendigo and I would still have business to settle. The mother wasn't going to forgive the death of the father and the scent of Dorothy's funeral pyre still stung in my nostrils. I might be able to get Valente out of this, but I was staying all in.

3

After an early afternoon breakfast, I started walking out towards the lake. The tracking spell was primed and ready. The lake was a good distance away and the wendigoes' lair was on the far side, so I hadn't pulled the trigger yet. I wanted to wait until I was a lot closer before I started pumping energy into the necklace. On top of that, I was still in the "city" and I'm not much for following around a pendant in public—at best, it gets me weird looks, at worst, somebody will come along with a torch and a rope.

What I really needed was a new set of wheels, since otherwise I had one very long walk ahead of me. I stopped by an ATM, drew out my daily limit, then went with one of my better tricks. I figured I had earned a little good karma and it probably wouldn't kill me to take out a line of credit on a luck spell. I closed my eyes and focused on the result I had in mind, me sitting behind the steering wheel. "Father, I could use a little luck here. Show me the way to go so that what you want can happen. Amen." Not exactly high magic, I grant, but it had helped me before in the past. Luck magic is dangerous if you don't invoke a greater being to govern it.

No voice thundered out of Heaven and no cars fell from the sky, so I started walking again. This kind of spell was subtle: no flash, no kaboom. It would work, though, provided I paid attention to whatever help Heaven offered. I had gone five blocks before a sign caught my eye: Redwind Drive. Not many street signs spell out words like avenue, boulevard, or drive. I took that as my sign and hooked a left on to Redwind Drive.

The road twisted off to the right through a slice of modern suburbia. The houses were nice, but not luxurious. A few people were out mowing their lawns, quite possibly for the last time until spring. A pair of kids were playing with a large dog, though I couldn't quite make out who was chasing who. I wandered slowly forward, keeping my eyes open, without looking like a burglar casing a job. The street went on like this for fifteen minutes. I was starting to feel like I had missed something when I saw her.

An older man stood in his driveway, bent over the hood of a midnight blue 1964 Ford Mustang. From the way his elbow was pumping, he must have been polishing a blemish out of the wax. It couldn't have been a very big flaw; she practically beamed in the afternoon sun. I strolled closer before calling out, "She's beautiful, sir."

The man turned and grinned, a gray mustache above his lip. "Thank you." He looked around at the other yards. "At least, I assume you mean the car. Never know when one of those neighbor girls is going to get it in their head to sunbathe."

"Even if there was a girl, she'd have to be quite a looker to compare to a first production year Mustang."

He cocked his head, a hint of frustration creeping over him. "My nephew posted that ad? I told him I didn't want to sell her that way. Internet, bah."

I laughed, wondering just how much good karma I'd spent on this one. I looked up and down the street to make sure there were no buses heading my direction. "No, sir, no Internet, just a Ford man. She's…well, I'm sure I've never seen one in such good shape."

"Well, that she is. I always wanted one when I was young. Couldn't afford her till I was well past the middle of the road. Probably for the best. How anyone survives to be older than twenty-one, I'll never know. I would've wrapped her around a tree when I was a kid."

I walked up the driveway to get a better look. "That would have been a shame…both for her and the tree. A car like that can give an oak a run for its money."

"That's true. She's all-American steel." He wiped his hands on the edge of the towel before extending his right hand. "Steve Daniels."

We shook. "Colin Fisher." If he wasn't worried about giving me his name, I wasn't worried, either. "Ad? You're not thinking of selling her, are you?"

"I'm afraid so. My wife and I are moving. Costa Rica. Beautiful place, but not for her. They drive like maniacs down there…and tax you a fortune to import an American car."

I started to reach out to pet her, then thought better of it. "You mind?"

He nodded. "Not at all." His eyes stayed on me as I ran my hand along the edge of her frame. My nerves were electric at the connection. There was luck and then there was Luck. I did a double-check in the sky for any signs of falling asteroids.

"You sure you didn't come about an ad?"

"I'm sure. I'm in the market, but …" I hesitated. "You're not going to believe this, but I just prayed for help in finding a car."

His eyes stayed hard on me, then relaxed. "That's where you're wrong. I think I do believe it. I've been asking God to show me the right person to sell her to. I can't stand the thought of someone driving her who doesn't love her the way I do. Do you need her, Mr. Fisher, or just want her?"

"Need. My Dorothy…I mean, my old car…was stolen." I didn't care for lying to the man, but, a believer in prayer or not, trashed by supernatural beasties was probably more than his belief, or his heart, could handle.

He nodded. "How much can you afford?"

"I've got five thousand on me. Whatever else you want, I can get when the banks open tomorrow." It wasn't a great car-buying strategy to issue a blank check, but I was in love. Dorothy was family, like an old aunt who could cuss and talk about new movies, but still knew how to bake cookies and make chicken soup. The Mustang was more like the head cheerleader in high school.

"Five thousand will be just fine. I'm not one to argue with God." He pulled a leather keychain from his pocket. "You want to take her for a test drive first?"

I smiled and pulled out my wallet. "I'm not much for arguing with God, either. If you say she runs, that's good enough for me."

We spent another half-hour looking her over. Steve showed me what he had done and what he thought might need to be done next and when. We swapped car stories, signed the title over, and fawned over her. As I was getting ready to leave, he asked, "What are you going to call her?"

"What did you call her?"

He shook his head. "It doesn't work that way. She probably means something different to you than she did to me."

I couldn't very well call her Dorothy; not only was that name taken, it was too old for her. Never mind that this car was twenty-two years older than Dorothy, the Mustang was eternally young. That though made me think about the dog-eared paperback I had read while working at the renaissance fair in Georgia. I'm probably the geekiest man alive for reading science fiction while pretending to be a medieval court wizard, but the name from Heinlein's book fit. "Dora. Adorable Dora."

4

I don't know how "adorable" she was, but she certainly handled like a spaceship. I thought the V8 in Dorothy was powerful, but Dora was at least a couple hundred pounds lighter with an even bigger engine. At five grand, I had gotten a bargain. I drove back to my hotel, loaded up a few extra things into the car, and took off for the vicinity of the lake.

I mostly behaved myself until I got off the Interstate. I had the country road between I-40 and the lake to myself and used the open space to put Dora through her paces. Truth be told, she put my driving skills to the test. She was everything I could handle and then some. I closed the gap between Interstate and gas station in under five minutes.

Rather than going the rest of the way to the lake, I pulled off into a back corner of the honky-tonk bar's gravel parking lot. I activated the waiting spell I had started earlier on the pendant necklace, then hung it around Dora's rearview mirror. As expected, the pendant leaned slightly toward the southeast. I took the road going east from the gas station, now at speeds within both reason and law. Every time a side road turned off to the right, I glanced up at the pendant, trying to judge if it was pointing more east or south.

I was driving for a half-hour at least before I decided to head south. I might have taken the turn before that one, but the road was dirt only and I wasn't eager to get Dora dirty just yet. She was far too pretty for off-road mudding. The one I turned on was gravel, but it looked like fairly well maintained gravel. I followed it for ten minutes before the surrounding woods began to peter out. I stopped at an old hippie commune…or at least, I guessed that's what it used to be. The man who met me at the entrance said it was a drug rehab center. From the way he talked, he suspected I was either a potential client or a connection trying to supply one of his current patients. I told him my only addiction was Middle Eastern oil and thumbed back at Dora. I think that relaxed him a little bit. I told him I was trying to find an old Native American friend, but had lost the directions she had given me. I don't know if he completely bought it, but he was helpful enough to point out the way to a place he thought she might be.

When I climbed behind the steering wheel, I thought I knew where I was going. That should have been a warning sign of impending doom, but I figured I was safe—it was still warm and sunny out. As I continued south, if I ever noticed the motorcycle in the distance behind me, I didn't process that it had been following me for quite a while now.

5

F ollowing the directions from the drug counselor, I found the Old Ways compound. It too looked like it might once have been a hippie commune, but its residents had been more fervent in redecorating. It didn't look like anything out of a John Wayne movie, but I was certain it was authentic Native American style that had been superimposed upon the original structures. A wooden sign out front simply said, "Old Ways," bracketed between two different tribal mandalas.

The place didn't feel right. There were no official signs indicating that I had driven on to tribal land and I didn't see anything indicating a tribal name. A lot of Oklahoma was tribal land, but most of the tribes proudly proclaimed their sovereign territory and posted the tribe's name everywhere and on everything. The style may have been authentic, but it wasn't natural: elements from eastern tribes, Great Plains tribes, northern tribes, and Aztec culture had all been blended together in one great mish-mash. The lack of antennas, satellite dishes, and other cars was also suggestive evidence that the residents here were "off the grid." I had met a lot of good people who lived that way, but they tended to be more than a little suspicious of outsiders and had their own laws regarding the use of violence.

I checked the pendant, then dismissed the spell with a grunt. It had been steadily pointing directly at a converted farmhouse five hundred yards off from where I was parked. The back half of the house had been redone in adobe and was covered in pictograms, feathers, wind chimes, and dream catchers. It looked like a peyote adventure as envisioned by someone on LSD, minus the psychedelic colors. It was the place all right, but I really didn't like the setup. I had been hoping for a trailer park or an old woman living all alone. Here, I was outnumbered a hundred to one, and all one hundred were staring out at my car. I knew Dora was sexy, but I doubted that was the way they felt about her intrusion.

I tucked my athame into the inside pocket of my leather jacket, then stuffed the two things I thought I might need for diplomatic negotiation into a small backpack. As I got out of the car, every eye in the compound shifted from Dora to me. There were a lot of people here for an off-road camp with no vehicles in the parking lot. Most were very old or very young, but the handful of adult males were on their feet as soon as I started walking. I didn't see any guns, but there were an awful lot of knives and axes laying around. The men's clothing was as contradictory as the buildings: worn, modern blue jeans with shirtless leather vests on top, decorated in tribal fashion. Some wore moccasins or sandals; the largest, a pair of Doc Martins.

I did what I always do when I was a stranger in a strange land—I walked in like I owned the joint. Nine times out of ten, a confident strut was as good as an all-access pass and would get me past most bouncers and security guards. This was apparently number ten for me. I was still a hundred yards from the house when I realized I was surrounded. Five men, mostly my age, flanked me. None of them looked happy to see me.

The biggest had four inches and fifty pounds on me, which is saying something as I'm not exactly short. He spoke in Cherokee, mostly to his companions. "Rabbit looks lost. Rabbit should not be in wolf's den uninvited."

I answered in Cherokee. "My presence is a question for the wolf-mother. I ask you to let me through." I figured I had started with swagger and there was no reason to change tactic now.

I couldn't have shocked him more if I had slugged him in the jaw. Despite the hair, battle injuries, and tanned skin, I imagine I still look like an upper-class East Coast white boy. Hearing his language coming from my lips must have been a near fatal shock. When he recovered, he nodded to me, then to the others, and switched to Spanish. "Keep him here, I will see what she says."

He left and the other four closed ranks. It was intimidating, but I did my best not to let it show. Less than five minutes passed before the big one returned escorting an old woman. Her dress was picturesque shaman and she reminded me of some of the Seminole pride paintings I had seen in Florida. When she appeared, my guardians parted, forming a half-circle behind me, separating me from my escape route to Dora.

She looked me over and I resisted the temptation to fork a ward against the evil eye in her general direction. When she spoke, it was in a language I couldn't quite place, but could understand anyway. "Little peyote boy, you looking for mystery, excitement. Curse you, boy." Then she spoke in English. "What do you want?"

"How do I know what she said?" I wondered at my inner voice.

"No idea. I can't place it. I'm not sure it has a name."

"Can I speak it?"

"Of course. But be careful. Not a lot of modern words to it. If you try for telephone or airplane, I have no idea what will come out."

I took a deep breath and went for it. "I would prefer if you did not curse me, wolf-mother."

I surveyed the impact. None of my guardians seemed to understand the language, but they all recognized it as her magic tongue. She understood me just fine, but didn't like it one bit. Her eyes narrowed to slits. "How do you speak the Old Tongue, boy?"

"I am full of surprises, wolf-mother. Your pups should know that by now."

She paused and her tone was slightly softer when she spoke again. Only slightly, like she would have preferred me suffering, rather than decapitated. "What do you want with me?"

"Peace, wolf-mother. I want peace. I want you to unspeak a curse."

She cackled. "Peace? Yes, white man always want peace. Piece of this, piece of that. What should I unspeak, white boy? I always speak truth."

"I am white, yes. But I am not the one who lets loose that which should not be disturbed. I am not the one who broke the peace of the Twins. The wendigoes are not a toy."

"What do you know about Hungry Winter, boy? You don't look hungry to me. And you people should not have woken Valente. You called demons first."

"Perhaps. But I could get Valente to acknowledge wrong, to make reparations. Whatever he has taken can be given back. Can you bring Hungry Winter to pay reparations? To put hearts back in chests? They know only violence, death, and hunger."

"Can Valente? My sons die to his poisons. There is no payment for life, only blood. Hungry Winter knows this: you either dine on the strength of your enemies or they will eat your life piece by piece. Hungry Winter will eat you, boy. You come because you fear for your master. Fear is good. Blood is better."

"Fear?" Anger crept into my face. I unzipped the bag. "No, I am angry. They murder innocents, people who work for a faceless entity. You think that boy up the road had ever met

Valente?"

"He spread his poisons, that is enough. And what innocent others? They all took land that was not theirs and lived on gold that should have been ours. And you fear. You fear, so you come to talk. White man's talk is hollow. My people know this."

I pulled out the wendigo head and tossed it at her feet. "I do not fear, wolf-mother. Hungry Winter is strong, but I am Winter Slayer." My voice rose in an attempt to overawe her. "Unspeak it, wolf-mother."

She stared at it in disbelief. I could tell, in that moment, she had never seen the wendigo in the flesh before. Dreams, perhaps, but seeing her great spirit champion reduced to a bloody trophy was world-shattering to her. When she spoke again, it was in Spanish. "White devil. I will deliver your head to your master."

The young men may not have followed our conversation, but they definitely understood that. Before I could react, both of my arms were pinned. The big one reached for an ax and headed my way. I could see the way this was going. If some devil wanted me to trade my soul for some practical combat magic, I would have considered the offer.

There was a pop, like a water balloon bursting, from somewhere behind me. The only sense I could make was that they were getting the champagne ready to celebrate my demise. Then, my right arm jerked forward as the man holding it dropped to his knees, screaming in pain. I stared down at him, not understanding why his left knee had picked that moment to explode.

"Gentlemen," a voice called out in English behind me. "Please let go of the white devil or my next shot will go through someone's collar bone. After that, it's all heads, hearts, and groins until I run out of ammo. Are we all on the same page?" Then, in Spanish, "Do you understand the words that are coming out of my mouth? Heads, hearts, and groins, not necessarily in that order."

Three of them apparently did, backing off rather quickly while raising their hands. The big guy with the tomahawk didn't. He rushed and swung, but the blow never landed. There was another soft pop, followed by an angry red gash in his lower right shoulder. In the instant between, it felt like a large, loudly buzzing bumblebee had just darted past my left ear.

"You want to try that again, Tonto? I don't care how much you think the devil's body is blocking my line of fire, it ain't. Don't fuck with me."

I stood shock still, not entirely sure what was going on behind me. The voice, vaguely familiar, spoke again. "Who is she, wizard? Why's she want you dead? I mean, other than general principles...you can be a little annoying."

"She cursed Valente and she's unhappy that I cut off the head of one of her curses."

"Oh." Pause. "Well, that changes things from personal to professional." I hoped she wasn't about to join the Valente Haters bandwagon. If she did, I was definitely repaying the borrowed luck from Dora. Her next question was a pleasant, almost lucky, surprise. "Do you need her alive for anything?"

The voice was high-pitched and sweet, capable of talking about killing someone without sounding dark or morbid in the least. Somehow knowing who was behind me didn't make me feel much better. "No need to hurt her. She was just about to unspeak the curse, weren't you, wolf-mother?"

She spat again. "Never. May the winter take all of ..."

She never got to finish that sentence before the bullet caught her on the nose, punching her face inward.

Veruca Wakefield called from behind me. "I'm the curse of Lucien Valente, fuckheads. You understand? Pay attention. Some curses are stronger than others."

6

V eruca and I had driven for fifteen minutes when she broke the silence. "You okay, Colin?"

I wasn't. The wolf-mother had been a spiteful old woman who had ordered my execution. Still, watching her die like that was something I wasn't prepared for. I lied. "Yeah, I'll be okay."

Veruca knew better. That's why she was driving Dora. Clearly, killing people was a normal day's work for her. She had calmly walked up to the body, verified the woman's death, and retrieved the wendigo head, all while keeping one long, sleek-barreled gun out and at least one eye on the rest of the tribe. As she escorted me back to my car, I had the feeling that she was accustomed to being horrifically outnumbered in hostile territory. She was all professional. I was shaking so badly that I couldn't open the driver's side door. Veruca took the keys.

As we drove past a pink and black rice-burner, she cursed, pulled out a keychain remote combo, and pressed a series of buttons. A loud explosion echoed out behind us as we sped away. "Third bike this month. Lucien is going to start docking my pay."

I think I grunted in response. Words weren't an easy thing

for me.

"Not a killer, huh? Can I ask what you expected to happen?"

I shrugged. "I don't know. Not that. I thought she'd see I had killed one of the wendigoes and fold."

Veruca shook her head, a lone scarlet bang whipping around freely, while the rest of her raven feather hair was pulled back into a tight ponytail. "My guess: from her perspective, she and everyone she knew had been folding for a long time. People like that, once they decide they're all in, they're done folding. Nothing you said could have changed that."

I didn't like it, but I suspected she was right. "She spoke of poison…I wonder if it was all about drugs. Maybe she lost someone to a drug addiction. Whatever or whoever it was, it changed her. She broke all of her people's laws, the peace of the Twins, by calling up the wendigo." I paused as I reflected on how stupid I had been to go there alone. "There was no going back after that."

"Yeah, you should have been more careful. Though to your credit, you looked like you were doing all right up until the end there."

"I suppose. What do you think the rest of them will do? Call the cops?"

"I doubt it. I suspect they hate the police as much as they hate Valente. My guess is they pick up stakes and move some place else. Maybe split into three or four groups under new leadership. They've been rousted before."

"And if they do call the cops?"

She shrugged. "What are they going to say? You didn't give them your name, did you? There were no security cameras posted, so the cops would need an eyewitness and forensics to nail us." The way she said the word "eyewitness," it sounded sarcastic, as if witnesses were a hard thing to come by where Lucien Valente was involved. I thought about asking what would happen if one of them did go to the cops and decided I really didn't want to know.

She picked up the conversation again while debating which way to turn at the next intersection. "So how did you find them? Lucien spent a lot of money trying to find out who sent that letter."

"Tracking spell." I tapped the necklace, now hanging limply from the mirror. "Used the letter and a little bit of the wendigo's blood to back track her."

"Not bad," she said. "You must know your stuff. I keep telling Lucien he needs to use his connections to hire one of the military sorcerers, but he has this idea that he knows how to find his own talent. I don't think he'd trust the government not to plant one of their own people in the Inner Circle. Maybe Lucien does know how to pick out fae bloods, demon bloods, and psychics, but wizards are a tough commodity these days. A lot of people talk the talk, but not many can walk the walk."

Fae bloods, demon bloods, and psychics...the phrase bounced around in my head, especially the plural "s" on the end of each word. Duchess Deluce wasn't the only more-than-human coworker on the payroll. Out of survival instinct, I threw up my trusty shell spell. "So which are you? And how did you find me?"

"No tracking spell, just followed you from your hotel. I owe you Burger King, remember? Oh, and nice moves, by the way. Picking up the wheels from the old man, you nearly shook me. Anybody else, you would have lost them. I figured you were staying on foot and was waiting for you at the end of the road, then you come whipping by in a souped up hotrod. Did you spot me or do you just normally assume you're being followed?"

I didn't want to strike her as a complete idiot, and she had dodged my question, so I fudged. "Well, I'm a little on edge after having my old car totaled last night."

She nodded. "You're learning quick. You've got to be a little paranoid to make it in this company."

I laughed, which bothered me. I shouldn't have been able to laugh at anything right then. "I should've known there was a catch when I saw the size of the paycheck." Pause. "So what do you do for Lucien?"

She pulled the car to a stop on the shoulder of the road, then turned to face me. "You really don't know? Duchess just said to call me and you called?"

I sized her up. She was all of five-one and looked younger than me by a couple of years. She didn't have the raw beauty of Miss Deluce, but there was a certain sexual energy about her. Her choice of clothing, and the bright red bang, confirmed my opinion that she was of my cohort: yet another rebellious twenty-something that didn't quite know where she fit into 21st century America. She was either the world's best shot or she had repeatedly risked my life back at the Old Ways compound. I pondered the pieces and didn't come up with much of anything that resembled a job title. I shook my head. "Nope. All I've met so far from the company is Lucien and Duchess. Haven't had the welcome to the company orientation yet."

"I'm Lucien's personal assassin." Her look dared me to laugh. I didn't laugh.

"Hubba hubba. I think I'm in love."

"You pick the weirdest times to come to the surface."

"Hey, I'm still tired from last night, but I'm not dead. I mean, she's sexy."

"She's also a professional killer, which likely implies lots of psychological problems, if not outright psychopathy."

"Like I said, sexy."

7

I f eating with Duchess at McDonald's had been surreal, the dinner at Burger King with Veruca was just downright bizarre. I would to have to expand my dining tastes if I was going to be hanging with this crowd. To an outsider, we undoubtedly looked like we belonged here. We wore the right clothes (leather jackets, t-shirts, jeans for me, electric blue leggings for her), appeared the right age (early to mid-twenties), and ate normal food (double cheeseburgers, fries, and shakes). But there was nothing, absolutely nothing, normal about the wizard and the assassin that were eating at our table.

Veruca dropped a trio of French fries past her bubblegum pink lips. Unlike Duchess, she had no trouble being awkward in public and spoke while chewing. "So how did you kill a wendigo if you don't have any cool combat spells?"

My tongue was getting me in all kinds of trouble with Veruca already. She was really attractive, highly flirtatious, and utterly disarming in person, unlike her deranged hermit act on the phone. I had just witnessed her job qualifications firsthand and as alarming as they were, I was still taken in by her bubbly, valley girl public persona. I had thanked her for the rescue back there, but my mouth kept on moving with all sorts of things I had no business telling her. This time I tried to restrain myself and kept my answer short, the better to make me sound cool. "Dagger. Exploding candles. Finished it with a katana."

Her eyes lit up. I would describe their color, but it wasn't possible. They changed like a mood ring on an acid trip. "Cool. I know a little Aikido myself. I may have to get you on the mat some time and see what you've got. But no magic?"

"The candles." Brooding quiet just wasn't my style. "I had setup the area as a magical sanctuary ahead of time. Gave me home field advantage and the ability to do some things I normally couldn't."

"Wicked cool. Most of Lucien's wizards have been totally lame. They wouldn't know how to set up home court, let alone use it to kill a werewolf."

"Werewolf? Not exactly. It's more of a spirit thing. It just takes the form of either a wolf or a blizzard."

"Oh." She took a big bite of her burger. "When you said wendigo, I figured you meant like from that werewolf game. Still...wicked cool."

"You're pretty wicked cool yourself," I said casually, mentally editing out any additions such as "for a stone cold killer".

"Stone cold fox, you mean."

I ignored him, a feat made possible by Veruca asking me a question. "So how did you get into the wizarding business? I mean, you're not born that way, right?"

I eyed her over my shake. "You were born into the assassin business?"

She switched to speaking in French. "Not so loud, sweetie. Your profession may not be a crime anymore, but mine still is. And, no, not exactly born into it. The Army made me a killer. Birth just gave me the tools to be the best."

I tried to keep a straight face, having picked up that she really disliked being laughed at. "You were in the Army?"

"Yeah. I made it into Cell Thirteen, but they decided I wasn't military material: I don't take orders well." She finished off her burger. "Protocol said they were supposed to kill me, but the guy they sent to do the job thought I was cute and hesitated a half-second too long. I knew about Valente from Cell Thirteen's file on him and applied for a job the next day. Not even the government is eager to tangle with him, not over one measly little assassin. And you …." She jabbed a fry at me for emphasis. "Dodged my question. How did you become a wizard?"

"A book," I said quietly. "A very special, very evil book."

She started to laugh, but stopped when she realized I was being serious. "A book?"

I nodded. I had never said it out loud before, but I wanted to with her, for reasons that went beyond sheer animal magnetism, though that was probably part of it. I confessed. "The Necronomicon. It ate my fiancée, I think. Afterwards, after she disappeared, I was changed."

"And we're not just talking grief, either. You mean something changed who you were, what you were capable of." Oddly enough, she sounded as if she understood.

"No, it wasn't grief. I knew things. Most of it was little stuff: good intuition, improved memory recall…but some of it…I had been studying Latin at school, but suddenly I could read it fluently. Then I discovered I could read anything; Every language ever known to man and a few that aren't, like the tongue that old woman was using."

She switched the conversation to Portuguese. "Weird, ain't it? I couldn't even follow that one, but I was born with a gift for languages…I can't imagine suddenly having all that thrust on to you."

"Yeah, but it doesn't stop there. I just…I knew magic. When

I read a spell book, I know what parts the author intentionally left out to thwart unworthy students. Heck, nine times out of ten I can come up with a better formulation than what they're advocating. Most of what I've picked up since then has just been my conscious mind catching up with what my subconscious already knows. Not a bad trade, right? The love of your life for phenomenal cosmic powers."

I should've stopped talking several sentences back, but I didn't. Veruca got up, then slid in next to me, her arms wrapping me up as best she could. "I am so sorry."

Taking comfort from a trained assassin didn't seem right, but I had trouble remembering just how dangerous she was. I tried to think of her as Veruca, rave girl, and found her embrace much more to my liking. "No need to be sorry, Veruca. You didn't do anything."

When she spoke again, it was in Cantonese. "No, but I can imagine what it's like. My great-great grandfather made a pact, too. That's where I get my demon's blood from."

"You know things, too, huh? From a demon's pact?"

"Some. Not as much as you. I didn't make the pact myself, but it lingers in the seed for a long time. It's never as strong in the children as in the first generation, though. I just learn languages really, really easily and have reflexes to make a cat jealous. Well, and a neat trick I can do with my hair."

She had switched to Italian and I answered in kind. "I didn't make a pact, at least, not on purpose. It was an accident: I said the wrong words at the wrong time." I could almost taste Sarai's blood on my lips again from our last kiss. "And I don't think it was with a demon."

"No, not demon. I can usually recognize my distant cousins on sight." Her Hebrew was spot on, complete with guttural stops.

"I'm sorry. I didn't mean—" She cut me off with a pair of

fingers to my lips.

"I know you didn't. Look, you probably shouldn't tell any of this to anybody else at the company."

"Why?" We were speaking in Russian now. "I mean, it's not like I advertise. You're the first person I've ever told any of that to."

"Because it bothers you. I can tell you think of yourself as a basically good person and it drives you nuts to think you might have hurt someone, even accidentally, just to gain power. It's a weakness. A nice weakness, sure, but the rest of them will use it against you...the Inner Circle of Lucien Valente isn't about being a good person. Heck, I'd probably use it against you, except I think you're kind of cute. You'll have to tell Duchess, though. She has ways of digging it out of your head."

"Not mine. I kicked her out."

Veruca hugged me tighter. "Perfect. Can you teach me? I've been wanting to get that bitch for months, but how do you screw over someone that can read your thoughts? Wait, later on that." She looked up at me with eyes that were shifting from magenta to emerald. "Look, I like you, Colin. If you'll let me, I'd like to see that you survive as personal wizard. But I need you to help me by pretending to be as tough as you can be. Play up your magical prowess and act like as much of a bastard as the rest of them whenever anyone is watching. Can you do that for me?"

"I can." I stared down at her and ran my hand through her black hair, playing it lose from the elastic holding her ponytail. It was soft as silk and cool to the touch. "But why? Why do you want to help me?"

She nuzzled against me and answered in Greek. I doubted I had ever heard a sexier tongue. "Because I told you I'm demon's blood and you didn't pull away from me. Didn't even flinch. If you can handle my inner monster, maybe I can handle yours."

"Handle me, baby, handle me."

"I can live with that." I scratched the back of her neck through her hair and she purred. "So before I get too worked up, are you seeing anyone?"

"Yeah," she confessed, and my heart sank. "Just started about five minutes ago. He's kind of a dork, but I've got a good feeling about him."

I pinched her. "Drama queen. Could you have made that pause any longer?"

"Maybe I was distracted," she replied in German.

"By what?"

"Well, I've got swearing down in every Indo-European language and I find it wholly satisfying."

"But?" I queried.

"I'm wondering how good I'll be at pillow talk with no language barrier. I may need you to teach me the right words."

"*Cha-ching.*"

I looked down at her and felt all kinds of things I thought I had forgotten how to feel. One of them stuck out above the rest and nearly forced me to tears as the knowing, the terrible knowing, washed over me.

"What is it?" Concern spread across her face.

"Nothing. Just memories," I lied.

I held Veruca against my chest. I had flirted plenty, but I didn't let anyone close. It was natural, given how Sarai had ended, to be a little paranoid. Veruca could kick my ass all day, any day, every day. And yet, when I had looked at her just then, I knew with the absolute certainty of the Eye of Winter that someday I would kill her.

8

eruca stood in the bathroom doorway, her cellphone cradled next to her head. I sat on the edge of the bed, trying to follow half a conversation between her and our mutual boss. She had tried to convince me that her phone wouldn't blow up if I touched it, but I wasn't one to chance fate. From what I heard, she had updated him on the death of the curse woman, without saying anything she wouldn't want the FBI or NSA to hear. I suppose all assassins must have their own "clean" jargon, but it was still odd to hear. The way she spoke, I would have thought she was Valente's art buyer rather than his hitman, err, hit-woman.

"No, sir. The only statue I wanted would have forced me to buy the whole lot. I just bought the one painting and put bids in on two others."

Pause. I didn't get the whole statue part, but I supposed the painting stuff meant she had killed one and injured two more. Either that, or she really was his art buyer, too.

"They'll have to be shipped ground. The gallery was off-grid, regular hippie types. We may have tax problems. I doubt the gallery will file receipts with the IRS."

The Old Ways people didn't seem like the type to call the cops? If that's what she meant, I'd have to agree. At least a quarter of them looked like they might be illegal immigrants. Still, didn't everybody call the cops after a murder? This was Oklahoma, not South Central, or Bogotá. Then again, I didn't even see any lightbulbs out there, let alone telephone lines.

"Yeah, I had to have help finding the place. The cab driver was a real wiz."

Me?

"I'd have to check...Fisher Cabs, I think."

Definitely about me.

"I don't have to. He's still sitting out front waiting. It's hard to find a good cabbie in this state."

Veruca walked over to me, her hand outstretched to offer me the phone. "He wants to talk to you."

I shook my head. "I really don't do cell ...."

"This time you do. You don't say no to him." She held it up against my ear.

"Hello?" I grabbed the phone and Veruca draped her arm across my chest as she dropped down on the bed behind me.

"Mr. Fisher, I must say this is a surprise. Miss Wakefield is treating you well, I presume?" Lucien Valente's voice came through crystal clear.

"Yes, sir. Umm...but I don't know much about art."

He grunted. "Ignore all that. I keep trying to tell her that these phones can't be tapped, but old habits die hard. You can speak freely."

"Can't be tapped? Could they intercept the signal?"

"Only if they knew what they were listening for. I'm not an R&D guy any more than I am a magic guy, but the designer assures me nobody else on the planet is using this type. You can say whatever you want. How did you meet up with Miss

Wakefield? Last I talked to her, she was taking a few days vacation time."

I tugged at my collar and tried to ignore Veruca purring over my shoulder. "Miss Deluce bet me I couldn't conjure up her phone number. I called Miss Wakefield up and we hit it off, once I got past all the death threats."

"Called her? I wasn't aware she was carrying a regular phone. Let me talk to her again."

I slid the phone behind me. "Yes, sir." Pause. "Yes, this line." Pause. "No clue. Aren't you glad I'm still just your art buyer?"

She handed the phone back. Valente sounded both puzzled and irritated. "Fisher? How the hell did you pull that off? These things can only call each other, not regular phones."

My voice cracked as I responded. "Magic. I used a gremlin-built cellphone and told it I needed to talk to Veruca Wakefield, Inner Circle of Valente International. The fairies took care of the rest." Veruca nibbling on my neck was not making conversation easy.

The silence that followed was long enough to convince me my anti-cellular juju had caught up to me. But eventually Lucien said, "My compliments, Mr. Fisher. You used magic to find the woman who cursed me? Fairies help you with that as well?"

"No, sir. A basic tracking spell. Probability magic, actually. A lake spirit clued me in as to where to start looking, but the spell took over from there. Do you want the details?"

"No, Mr. Fisher. That won't be necessary. Do we owe the fae anything for the phone call or the tip?"

"No, sir. I don't get in debt with them. I pay as I go."

He sounded genuinely impressed. "Finally, a little competence. You wouldn't believe what the Seelies tried to charge me for a deal one of my past wizards made with them."

"Kids?" I guessed.

More silence. "Maybe you would believe." He paused. "So

where are we on the curse? Is it over?"

"No, sir. I killed one of the wendigoes, but it's a family: mother, father, and child. I took out the adult male."

"Are you sure it's dead? From what I know of most supernatural beasts, they are remarkably resilient."

I had to stifle a laugh as Veruca's fingers probed my ticklish vulnerabilities. "Yes, I'm sure. I took its head, if you'd like it mounted for a souvenir."

He did laugh. "I think I would. Tell Miss Wakefield to send it to me. She'll know where and how without attracting unwanted attention."

I relayed that to her. She huffed, but obediently hopped off the bed to find it. Valente continued. "Tell me how it died, Mr. Fisher, and what plans you have for the other two."

I did, though I was selective about what I said regarding Tia or the Eye of Winter. "That's about it, Mr. Valente. Duchess is setting up the company picnic for Tuesday night. I'm sure the wendigoes will want to eat, but they'll give my sanctuary a wide berth. I'll work out something else, though."

"No, you won't, Mr. Fisher. I think your role in this particular adventure is at an end."

I choked on that. "I'm fired?"

He chuckled. "No, quite to the contrary. You've proven too valuable an asset to risk in combat. Will any fire and steel suffice or is magical ground also a prerequisite to killing them?"

"Any fire and steel. You have to burn off the ice cloud that surrounds them. That makes them about as dangerous as any large wolf. But, sir…they're fast and they're good at sneaking up on people. They like to retreat if things aren't going their way. I wouldn't want to see Veruca try to take them alone."

"Veruca is likewise too valuable. I'm sending a Corporate Response Team to you. You will brief them and they will handle things during the party. Keep it simple for them, they are former military, but you don't have to pretend the wendigoes are just normal animals. They've faced supernatural-level threats before. Make sure the team understands their tactics, their tendencies, and the importance of fire and steel. The CRT will handle the rest."

"And then what?" Truth be told, I was a little disappointed. I still wanted a piece of the monsters for what they did to Dorothy.

"After you brief the CRT, come home to Boston. I need you here. I've needed the advice of a real wizard for some time now."

That prompted me to ask something that had been gnawing at me. "Sir, with all due respect, why did you hire so many fakes before me? I mean, I haven't heard Duchess or Veruca say a single nice thing about any of them."

"A valid question, Mr. Fisher. The fae courts insisted on it. They refused to treat with my emissaries unless they were wizards, something about ancient traditions to keep. Most of the talented ones are already in the employ of the military, so I had to make do with what I could find." The short silence that followed felt contemplative, as if Lucien was debating how much to tell me. "I can't afford to lose the fae courts, Colin. FBI, CIA, Interpol, they could turn on me and I could handle it. On the other hand, the faeries scare the hell out of me."

My mind returned to the forgotten whispers of the Eye of Winter. I shivered despite the heat radiating from Veruca's body. "Me too, Lucien. To tell the truth, I would think anyone who isn't frightened by them is either a liar or an idiot."

Veruca kissed my shoulder. "Let me talk to him, Colin."

His voice came from my other side. "I heard that. Put her on."

Veruca leaned back as she took the phone from me, but her legs snaked up around my stomach, preventing me from leaving or turning around to face her. She wasn't applying pressure, but I got the feeling she could make this hurt if she wanted to. "So are we keeping him?"

A second passed. "Good."

Another. "Absolutely. Not a doubt, sir. He's the real deal. He downplays himself, but I suspect he could go rounds with any of the guys Cell Thirteen is using."

This time Lucien's response must have been longer. "Understood, though I may have trouble getting him on the plane. He's a little bit technophobic…and he has a smoking car. It would be a shame to leave her here."

Her grip loosened, her big toe absently stroking my thigh. "Actually, sir, remember that favor you owe me? I'd like to collect. Let me act as his bodyguard whenever you don't need me elsewhere. I'll drive back with him and make sure nothing unfortunate happens to him."

I would've given the rest of my chocolate supply to hear whatever Valente said in response. "Yes, sir, that favor."

A pause. "It's not a little thing. Not to me."

The pause that followed nearly drove me insane. "Yes."

"Insanity is a short drive for us."

The phone appeared over my shoulder again. "He wants to say goodbye to you." Coming from his private assassin that phrase scared me, but I didn't feel in mortal danger.

"Yes, sir?"

Lucien's voice sounded deeply impressed. "We will talk when you get here, Mr. Fisher. Whatever it takes to keep you in my employ, it can be arranged."

"I already told you my terms, Mr. Valente. Freedom of conscience and Sarai. The paycheck is just the icing on top."

"I will have a file ready for you when you arrive with everything I can find on the girl. Do you need your second check deposited before you arrive?"

"No, sir. It can wait."

He laughed. "Sorry, that wasn't what I meant to ask. I'm

afraid Miss Wakefield has me a little flustered. Her request caught me by surprise…you haven't bewitched her mind, have you?"

"No, sir. I wouldn't. I think she just has that effect on people."

"She saved my life once." He paused to compose his thoughts. "Apparently, staying attached to you is worth my life, as she has decided to call in the debt. Is that acceptable to you?"

I turned around to face her and her upper thighs loosened their grip to let me. I stared down into her eyes, watching them shift from a silvery blue to a deep emerald. We each knew what the other was, but neither was pulling away. It wasn't love, but then again, maybe that's what love really is: knowing and staying anyway. I kissed her lightly on the lips, before bringing the phone back up to my mouth. "Yes, sir, that's acceptable."

9

T he room was darker when I woke up. Veruca must have drawn the curtains shut, because no evidence of the coming full moon penetrated into the room. I sat up, planning on stumbling blindly towards the hotel room's bathroom. That attempt at motion signaled to me just how much was horribly wrong in the room. I know, after the week I was having, I should have been quicker on the uptake.

Slender arms, not Veruca's, were clutching at me. The girl on the bed next to me was wide-eyed, the whites of her eyes bright with fear. By their pale light, I could make out a mess of blond curls framing a face too young to be sharing a bed with me. I renewed my efforts to sit up, but the bed under me was unstable. The girl fell into my arms. "Shh, Teddy. If we make noise, he might come back.

My vision flickered, blurred, as if I were looking beyond her for an aura. The world split in two and I was simultaneously a resident of both. In one, the tangible world where a little girl no more than twelve clung to me, I was not a man, but a dark-furred teddy bear with kind, round eyes, a sewn nose, but no mouth. In the other, the world where the bed had shifted and collapsed, I was me, but the bed was a pile of dead bodies. The frame had decayed into skeletons. The box spring was full of feminine corpses in varying stages of decay. All were older than the girl, but most were still younger than me. The mattress was a jumble of teenage beauty queens, all naked, most in the last stages of dying. It might have been easier on me if they had been dead, not gasping with putrid bursts for one last breath. The pillow the bear rested upon was, in this shadow world, a fifteen-year-old red head with a syringe sticking out of her jugular. If she was still alive, I was grateful she wasn't moving.

I stifled a scream. I sensed that if I did yell, it would mean horrible things for the child who held me. He would return and that would be bad, very bad. I tried to whisper to her, to tell her I would help, that I would get her out of here before the bad man could hurt her again. I couldn't; the teddy bear had no mouth. I struggled but I couldn't force out anything through those missing lips. By default, I did what teddy bears do: I held her.

It was a dream, just a dream. If I could just close my eyes and ignore the stench and the writhing, I would wake up in a hotel room in Oklahoma. It was just a dream.

"Not for them, my love. Not for her." I knew that voice. Somewhere between a dusky soprano and a high alto, hers was meant for romantic suspense on Broadway. Hearing it comforted me, confirmed the dream state, and yet simultaneously made the bed of corpses more solid, more real. Details of the girls' faces, skin tones, and manner of demise were noticeable now.

I answered in my that-realm voice, where the lips moved…if I could ignore the dying girl's hair in my mouth. I couldn't turn my head without breaking the physical link to the motionless teddy bear. "What's killing them? A serial killer?"

"Criminal neglect," Dream-Sarai answered. "I need you to listen, my love, my hope. Our time is short."

I took in a deep breath, pressed the stuffed animal closer to the girl, and closed my eyes. "Hurry."

"You won't save them, my love. Maybe you could, but you won't. You need to save her, though. Whenever you're distracted, whenever you're tempted to call it splits, remember the one clutching the teddy bear. Save her and the rest will be avenged at least."

"It's just a dream, Sarai. I'm a stuffed animal. How can I save her?" My voice was weak and tired, like I was speaking in the real world, but hearing the faint echoes of it in dreamland.

"It's real for her, my love. Her father is horribly abusive. Tomorrow, she will run away. The day after and the week after, there is nothing you can do for her. Even the year after, the world will still be a terrible place. But when the time comes, when she holds you again as she clutches you now—save her, save the world."

"Save the world?" I mumbled, more awake than asleep now.

"Save her. Even if you have to let me go to do it...save her. No matter what Lucien asks of you, no matter how dark and vicious the valley becomes, hold the course. Save her and we can finally rest."

When I awoke in the hotel room, the moonlight of the midnight hour was softly falling through the curtains. For a moment, I thought I saw Sarai standing there in the pool of silvery light. Then she was gone.

I stumbled into the bathroom. In the dark, I took care of business, then splashed water on my face while trying not to look into the mirror. The dead girls and, worse, the dying might be looking back out at me. On my way back, I checked to make sure the Necronomicon was safely tucked away. It was still in the same drawer, though the Gideon's Bible had disappeared. I eyed the vile book nervously, half-expecting it to burp out a single corner of a page, like the cartoon cat post-canary.

When I laid back down, a sleeping Veruca draped one arm over my bicep without waking. I had to bite down on my tongue not to scream. It had been a week like that, where even the best things got twisted.

10

T he CRT team leaders met us at an office building downtown the next morning. I didn't have much experience with the military mindset, but I was fairly impressed with what I saw. After talking to us yesterday, Lucien dispatched not one, but two, of Valente International's CRTs. Mr. Valente was committed to making sure wendigoes became an extinct species.

I had expected something different from a Corporate Response Team. The phrase made me think of spin doctors and ad executives. Given what they were sent to do, my brain married that image with upscale security guards. I would have been closer if I would have pictured Samuel L. Jackson playing a former military blacktops soldier turned private sector after an early retirement, then cloned multiple times. All six of the leaders struck me as being qualified to take over a third world country with a rubber band, a paper clip, and a few loyal followers.

The difficulty that concerned them wasn't so much the wendigoes as the presence of civilians. While Valente International was allowed by law to recruit, train, and equip any number of such CRTs, it was illegal for them to operate on U.S.

soil. They were worried about how to take down a pair of supernatural predators while attracting minimal attention from the nearby picnickers. I was worried about little things, like the wendigoes killing all of them.

In the end, it was decided that half of one team would go in plain clothes and form a loose ring outside the picnic. The rest would be in full tactical gear and spread out along the top of a hill north and east of the party area. I would arrange for Tia to lead the wendigoes through an open valley below it, but the CRTs were going to deploy thermal sensors throughout the woods in case my "inside man" proved less than reliable in getting the wendigoes into position. Valente told me to keep it simple, so I neglected to mention that my co-conspirator was an adolescent female lake spirit. I'm not sure which of those elements they would have found most objectionable, but I was sure they wouldn't like it.

I was glad to be done with it. I had been disappointed when Valente first pulled me out of the game, but I had both time to think about it and a night lying next to Veruca. One made me realize just how lucky I had gotten the first time around. The second made me feel like I still had something to live for. Dorothy would be avenged whether I was the one pulling the trigger or not.

The meeting did have one upside to it. I had been curious as to how their plainclothes men would have enough firepower to deal with a wendigo, if one managed to sneak through. I doubted they could carry a flamethrower and still look inconspicuous. Apparently, fire was a common enough job requirement for a Valente CRT that they were well ahead of me. One of them showed me a small black cylinder, only slightly larger than a can of mace. He insisted it was a single-use handheld flamethrower. Unless they were pulling my leg, and they didn't seem like the type to joke about anything (especially about weaponry), it produced a ten foot long cone for five seconds and would burn in excess of two thousand degrees. In short, it was easily twice as powerful as the burst I had called up through the candles and without any reference to magic.

I asked how I could get one, not really expecting a positive answer. The team leader surprised me by saying I could keep that one, so I did. If I ever ran into another wendigo, it would come in handy. No sooner did I slide it into my pocket then I wondered what I could get a gremlin to build for me if I traded the device off to him.

"Don't even think about it."

11

What bothered me the most was how perfectly it all went down. Tia didn't balk at the yellow and purple polka-dot beach umbrella I brought her in payment for her wendigo-baiting services. I got the feeling that either my fight with Hungry Winter or my conversation with the Eye of Winter had impressed her to the point that she wasn't likely to try anything slick with me again.

No tourists or park rangers stumbled along at the wrong moment to discover a small army setting up on the hill. No random meteors crashed down out of the sky on Dora. There wasn't a single pimple on Veruca's face. I wished there would have been. It would have relieved me to know that not everything was going our way. As rough as it had been for me lately, I found it impossible to believe that fortune favored me completely.

Technically, Veruca and I should have been cruising down the road in Dora, possibly on the other side of Tulsa, heading toward the Missouri border. But while neither of us was clamoring for a spot on the front lines, we both wanted to be there in case something went horribly wrong. Besides, it was a Valente company picnic and we were Valente employees. Given all of the subsidiaries involved, I doubted anybody would notice we weren't locals. We mingled and ate hot links, all the while keeping one ear open for the sound of gunfire. I had a digital thermometer and kept checking the ambient air temperature around me, but there were no unnatural dips, just the slow, steady progress of night.

Nothing happened. Around midnight, a pair of men tried to fight each other, but they were both far too drunk to be any good at it. One of the plainclothes I recognized from the setup meeting broke it up with little more than a flick of the wrist and a stiff arm. By one o'clock, it was down to just us and the plainclothes.

I walked up to the one who had played peacemaker. "I guess they decided not to show up. We go to all this trouble …."

He held up one hand, then placed the other over his ear wick. When the hand came back down, he said, "Actually, sir, we did. We killed one and wounded the other. The out team is following its blood trail to ground to finish the job."

"What? When did they show up? Why weren't we notified?" I had a sickened image of the female wendigo dragging around a wounded animal in its teeth to create a fake pathway of vitae. It was smart enough to plan an ambush of its own.

"Two hours ago, sir. And there was no need, sir. Your plan went over near-perfect. No injuries, no civilian encounters."

I felt like stealing a line from Rambo, something about his men already being dead, but maybe I was just punch-drunk on paranoia. Before I could think of anything better to say, his hand returned to the ear wick.

"It's over, sir. Out team called in. They're both dead."

I tried to smile for his benefit. To me, it still felt very far from over.

FOURTH INTERLUDE

arrie Ann Womack edged her way closer to the Hispanic man. She was traveling alone, but didn't want to look like she was alone. The middle-aged man appeared to be by himself, too. Carrie didn't know what she would do if a plump wife and a pack of children suddenly appeared from the bus stop restroom.

She had thought about taking a Greyhound before, but it was different today. Today, she had courage. She bought two tickets from the Asheville station to New York City. Either the clerk believed her when she said her dad and her were going to visit his sister or the clerk didn't really care. Somehow, she thought he would've cared if she had said she was an unaccompanied minor. Adults had the funniest ideas about what eleven-year-olds could and couldn't do.

Carrie wasn't old enough to travel all the way by herself, but she was going to, whether Greyhound said she could or not. She wasn't supposed to have to deal with abusive adults at her age, but that hadn't stopped the drunken slob who used to be her dad. He was still passed out when she left for school that morning. Carrie had looted his wallet and discovered he had just gotten paid the day before. He didn't keep jobs long enough for her to figure out the pay schedule, but luck was with her. She took it all instead of the usual five she sneaked when he wasn't looking, then doubled back to her room to add a change of clothes to her backpack. If her luck held, she'd be in the Big Apple by morning.

Carrie corrected herself: it wasn't luck. Her knight had come to her last night in her dreams. He hadn't been clad in shining armor, but in teddy bear fur. She couldn't hear what he was saying, but she knew why he had come: he was going to save her from the monster. That's what knights did. Every girl dreamed of a knight coming to her rescue, but she really had one. Of course, most girls she knew didn't really need rescuing.

It had been all right before Mom died. But the onset of her puberty, his growing alcoholism, and their mutual grief had twisted her dad into an evil dragon. She wanted to kill him, but that was a knight's job. Carrie's job was to run, to get away. Her knight would find her in New York.

She had seen TV shows about New York. They took care of kids there. They had detectives who investigated crimes about kids and lots of social workers who knew how to do their job. They'd put her with child services and the caseworker would believe her when she said her dad hit her. She didn't think the police in New York could arrest her dad in North Carolina, but she knew they wouldn't send her back. She would be safe with a foster family until her knight came to her. If she was really lucky, she wouldn't even need him when he did show up. She could take care of herself. Still, she would love him. He was a knight, after all, and his visitation had given her the confidence she needed to escape.

The bus came and Carrie walked on at the heels of the man she had temporarily adopted. The driver took their tickets, but didn't say anything. Carrie took a seat by herself on the row behind the pretend father. The rest of the day was spent studying the map she had purchased at the bus station and staring out the window. Carrie had escaped from the monster and was making her way to the fabled City of the North.

It wasn't marked on her map or on any of the road signs, but Carrie Ann Womack was heading straight to hell. It would be four years, six months, and two days before she would find herself sliding into an IHOP booth across from her predestined knight.

PART FIVE

SEASONS CHANGE

"Is the pen mightier than the sword? Maybe, maybe not. Size

doesn't always count for as much as you might think: I've seen a

goblin kill a dragon. Wait, the moral of that story is don't swallow

anything whole that's holding a spear. Still, it's not wise to judge a

book by its cover."

-Jadim Cartarssi, Off-topic Parabalist

1

"**N**ot bad for a newbie." By the sound of her voice, Veruca was clearly entertained. "The way you're spending money, a girl would think you had been rich forever."

"It's not my money," I said, defensively. "Besides, Lucien had most of this stuff lying around already."

She slid up beside me. Her long, lone bang was carnation pink today, a color that I'd come to associate with her being more playful than normal. "Relax, tiger. I think it's nice. I bet you could sling some serious magic in here."

I hoped she was right. Lucien Valente has opened up his checkbook to help me open up shop. Valente International Headquarters already had a ritual magic room, but it was located a floor below the company's servers and firewalls. To date, the *National Enquirer* had run three different stories about the specters Valente web surfers ran into the one and only day I was in said ritual room. After that, Lucien and I both agreed it would be best if I spent most of my time off-site.

Fortunately, Valente owned an abandoned motel through one of his subsidiaries. The first floor was being renovated for use as halfway house apartments for sex offenders, which had more to do with tax write-offs than charitable interests on Valente's part. They weren't exactly my first choice of neighbors, but their parole stipulated that they couldn't own or operate computers, much less have Internet access. I suspected the other reason Lucien picked this spot for me was that no one would miss my new neighbors if a ritual ever called for a human sacrifice or two.

"I knew I liked the guy for some reason. He's practical."

I ignored him. If that was on Lucien's mind, I didn't want to know. I was finding that applied to a lot of things when it came to my new boss: I didn't want to know.

"Because if you knew, you would have to do something about it. Damn hero complex."

"You said it."

"Ever thought about applying that principle to Sarai?"

"Shut up."

"Colin?" Veruca's tone was puzzled, suddenly cautious and curious. "Are you okay?"

I shook the cobwebs out of my brain and let my fingers wrap around her delicate hand. "I'm getting there. Just an old ghost in the machine."

"Really?" She perked up.

"No." I hoped. Surely it was just me in here, right? I looked her in the eyes. They were currently mint green, but slowly fading towards tan. They were easy eyes to get lost in.

"Liar." She pecked me on the cheek with her lips, then wrapped one leg around mine. We had enough sparring matches that I recognized my growing peril and shifted my weight to brace against the coming leg sweep.

Of course, we'd also sparred enough that I knew my preparations were utterly hopeless. "I yield, milady. I was just thinking that there are some things in life that I'm better off not knowing."

"I'm not sure which statement is smarter. I think you are better off knowing when I'm about to kick your ass." She kissed me again, this time on the lips.

I relaxed. I wasn't eager to crash down on the stone-tiled floor of my arcane laboratory. I was still sore from our morning workout and that was entirely done on padded surfaces.

The second floor of the motel was entirely de-walled, save where they were a structural necessity, making one big room out of what used to be twenty-four rooms. The shag carpeting and picture windows went out along with the interior walls. It still looked like there were windows from the outside, but they had all been plastered over, save for one on the western side and one on the eastern side. In the center of my roughly 7,200 square foot apartment, a flawlessly round silver circle had been embedded in the floor. I could have parked Dorothy inside the circle's nine-foot radius. I could probably squeeze two Doras in there, without either touching.

All that had been more or less to my specification, once Valente had asked me what kind of setup I needed. As soon as the remodeling was finished (I won't say how quickly he got it done; no one would believe me), the special deliveries began to arrive. Lucien had a rabid hunger for the supernatural and had accumulated thousands of relics and artifacts over the years. Those of known power and property were employed elsewhere throughout the company or were in Lucien's personal possession, but that left a large number of items that were suspected of being magical, but with propertus arcanus unknown.

Veruca and I were standing five feet from a prime example. The workers had constructed a display case to house two crossed identical spears. Supposedly, they were exact replicas of the Spear of Destiny, made by Hitler's henchmen after the original escaped their custody. The lives of their past owners were interesting to say the least, but whether it was because they owned the spears, or because they were weirdo freaks, remained to be seen. When I asked Lucien why he sent them to me, he said he thought they might be of more use to a Catholic wizard than to a Taoist CEO.

I thought they were creepy, but I was learning to pick my fights. If I was going to object every time Lucien Valente did something that bothered, frightened, or annoyed me, I might as well resign.

"So what's on the agenda for today?" Veruca queried.

"I'm not sure. There's a representative from the Unseelie court coming here to meet me tonight. The meeting's set for sundown, but I'm afraid I haven't checked the paper yet. Somewhere between six and seven. I should probably have some token of hospitality ready: a bottle of red wine, maybe. Lucien is sending me another batch of Jane Doe reports to sort through that loosely match Sarai's description. Other than that, not much. Anything you want to do?"

"Actually, I've got a job to take care of." She kissed me on the forehead. "It's been a fun month, Colin, but Mr. Valente still needs new art for his office."

"I don't want to know, do I?"

"Probably not. But I'll tell you if you ask."

I shook my head. "Not necessary, my love. When will I see you again?"

"Shouldn't take more than three or four days."

"Short job, huh?" I didn't know much about the murder-for-hire business, but I assumed it usually took weeks to properly plan and execute a job.

She laughed. "Not really. Most stateside jobs only take five or six hours. This one's international."

A whistle, low and somber, escaped my lips. "This isn't the first job since we've been back in Boston, is it?"

"Our boss has a lot of enemies, Colin. I figured you didn't want to know." She pulled a black velvet necklace box out of her back pocket. "I got you something to keep you company until I get back. A second bodyguard of sorts."

"A going away present, huh?" I opened it up, looked at it, turned it, looked at it again, and still had to ask, "What is it?"

"A 'til-I-get-back-you'd-better-not-get-yourself-killed present.

It's a chaos blade."

It looked like a letter opener made from soapstone. As I pulled it from its box, the crystal changed from off-white to limestone green. It didn't look like much, but I could feel the vibrant hum of magical energy throbbing from within it. "What's it do?"

"Like most weapons, the idea is to put the pointy end into the other guy." She took a couple of strides backward. "A chaos blade just lets you bring a few unexpected surprises to the party. It's like the AK-47 of the supernatural world: everybody's got one."

I raised an eyebrow. "This thing? Not much range to it, is there?"

Veruca brushed the carnation bang back out of her eye. "You'd be surprised. What's the wooden katana we practice with feel like in your hand? Try to imagine it."

I did. The letter opener, now a greenish-gold color, twisted in my hand until it was a sky blue duplicate of my three-foot long practice blade. Weight was no issue; it still felt as light as a nail file in my grip.

"Shrink it down to the size of a hairpin and you can walk it past any metal detector or full body scanner in the world. Some colors set off Geiger counters, but most don't."

"Some colors?" I mentally reshaped the blade to a large Scottish claymore. It stayed blue for half a second, then faded to muddy brown. Despite being six-feet long and three inches wide, it couldn't have weighed more than a few ounces. "Any way to control the color?"

"Nope," Veruca replied. "Or if there is, I've never heard of it. It's materialized chaos; it's not meant to be fully controlled. Color does matter, though: when you hit a target, it has extra effects based on the current manifested color."

I tried to pretend we were talking about a new video game and found the conversation a little bit easier to process. "Effects?

Like what?"

"Hard to tell ahead of time. If it's bright red or reddish orange, it will probably catch stuff on fire. But I wouldn't be surprised by anything that it does. The only firm rule is that when two of them go against each other, the first person to hit usually wins. For the size and price, there is nothing more deadly than a chaos blade in the hands of a creative user."

I gave the sword a couple of hesitant practice swings, being careful to avoid my girlfriend or any of the display cases. I'd never used anything like it, but it did exactly what I wanted it to, more like an extension of my own arm and will then a held object. "So accidentally poking myself through my jeans pocket would be bad?"

Veruca was smiling as she watched me test out my gift. "Maybe, but most likely not. You hear horror stories sometimes, but the blades seem to have a good sense of who they work for, who they belong to. I'd say that one likes you; it fits well in your grip."

I thought of something outside of the blade family, a spiked morningstar like something out of a cheesy B gladiator movie: overly large and visually menacing. The chaos blade went through something more like a baseball bat, before readjusting to fit my mental image, now a dazzling crimson. "I like it. Thank you, V."

I shrank it back down to a letter opener, then thought better of it and imagined an old school fountain pen. My gift cooperated and I slid it into my shirt pocket. Veruca walked up and looked me over. "Well, that's a new way to carry one. It suits you and your revamped wardrobe. Harvard dropouts just don't look right in jeans and a t-shirt."

"This from an assassin who never leaves home without something pink on?" Three weeks ago, I would've been too scared of her to use that particular barb, but I was evolving into my new life position. I had upgraded my clothing: a dark blue tailor-made long sleeved shirt and charcoal gray slacks. Only the leather jacket and steel-toed boots remained from my previous incarnation. I would be buried in both if I had any choice in the matter.

She planted a kiss on me. "I may wear pink, but at least I didn't get my ass kicked by a girl this morning. Don't skimp on the exercises: I expect you to be more of a challenge when I get back."

"What about Thanksgiving? Are you going to be back in time for my first attempt at cooking a turkey?" It was the Friday before, but I knew she was less than eager for the event.

"That depends. Are you using an oven or magic? Your sorcery I trust, your kitchen skills not so much."

Blow up one little microwave and no one lets you forget it.

2

After V left, I ran down to the liquor store to pick up a bottle of wine. I wasn't sure what was appropriate for an Unseelie ambassador, but Autumn Chill red seemed like it might do the trick. I splurged on a bottle of Kahlua and some high priced vodka just in case the fae wasn't a wine drinker…or in case I got lonely while Veruca was on assignment. Without the familiar comforts of road life, I found it harder and harder to sleep at night. If vodka was strong enough to help people survive Communist Russia, it would work for me, too.

I stopped by an ATM to see if my paycheck had made it into my account yet. Not that I was in any danger of going broke: with the next check, I would be approaching seven digits in the account. My check was in, so I went back into the bank and requested twenty grand (which they provided after another phone call to Valente's office), and separated it into two stacks. The first stack went into my wallet as mad money. The second I wrapped in plastic wrap, then in aluminum foil, and added it to the growing pile under Dora's spare tire. It would take some explaining in the event of a police search of my vehicle, but I knew I might not be a personal wizard forever. An escape fund could come in handy if Valente ever decided I had outlived my usefulness. I now had fifty grand squirreled away for a really bad rainy day.

"Rainy day? More likely the second coming of Noah's flood."

When I closed Dora's trunk, I was startled to discover I wasn't alone in the strip mall parking lot. Special Agent Rick Salazar leaned against the trunk of a sidewalk-encased tree. He had experienced a wardrobe change, too, in the intervening month: only the tan trench coat looked vaguely FBIish. Beneath it, he sported threadbare blue jeans and a white t-shirt. "Mr. Fisher."

I wondered how much of that process he had just witnessed. It wasn't illegal to store bricks of cash in the trunk of your car, but it wasn't normal, either. As I slowly walked towards him, I absentmindedly brushed the pen in my shirt pocket. "Agent Salazar. Is this an official visit?"

He shook his salt-and-pepper hair. "Furthest from. If anybody asks, I'm just leaning here, trying to remember my ATM code." He glanced around the parking lot furtively. "I'm not allowed to talk to you."

"Not allowed? The bureau's still convinced I'm a psycho?"

"No." He shifted the peppermint he was sucking on to the other side of his mouth. "Your employer. Nobody talks to Valente employees in a formal capacity without a warrant and the director's personal authorization."

That shook me. "Is Valente under investigation?"

"Don't know. Don't want to know. Either he has been for the last decade and we don't know enough to arrest him or he's bought the whole damn bureau from the deputy director level on up." He paused, clearly deliberating whether he should ask what he had come to ask. "Were you working for him last time we talked?"

"Nope. He hired me the morning after."

He nodded, his internal lie detector apparently satisfied. "Do you have a clue who you're working for?"

"The devil I know." That line drifted back to me from my first interview.

Salazar grunted. "Close enough. He's bad news, Mr. Fisher. I can sympathize with some terrorists: they believe that what they are doing is the right thing, at least within their own twisted logic. Lucien Valente...all he believes in is money and power. He'll sell weapons to the Israelis, then invent counter-measures to sell to the Palestinians, then upgrades to let the Israelis bypass the counter measures. Drugs, slaves, guns, brand-name clothing... he'll sell anything if the money is good."

"Nobody else wanted to pay for my skills. A man's got to make a living somehow."

"Like this?" Salazar thrust a manila envelope at me.

I looked inside and wished I hadn't. The contents were a stack of forty or fifty black and white crime scene photos. The people in them resembled the aftermath of a war, just waiting for the bulldozer to dig the mass grave. All of them were dead from the same wound: massive, gaping holes where their hearts should have been. I recognized a few of the faces despite slight decomposition, especially the large man with his right arm in a crude sling. The last time I had seen him, he had been trying to separate my head from my body via tomahawk. "The Old Ways. When?"

"Hard to tell. We didn't find them 'til more than a week later. Sometime between when you asked for directions at the drug rehab center and when you and Veruca Wakefield left town two days later."

I shot him my best tough guy look. "Are you sure this isn't an official interview?"

He shrugged. "You could tell me you killed all of them and I couldn't use a word of it in court."

"I didn't kill any of them."

"That's the damnedest part of it, you didn't. It would work so much better if you had. You found one of the bodies, you went to work for the victim's employer, heck, took over the victim's old job for all I know. I've got witnesses that show you were out there trying to find a group of people, who all just happen to get killed that same way a couple days later. The more I look at those pictures, the more those chest wounds look like what a really big animal maw would do to a human body...and your old car got tore apart by wild animals, then burned to slag, a few nights before they died. You leave town and the murders stop." He held up his hands in puzzlement. "If I found a guy who swore he saw you working as a lion tamer, I might have something that made half a lick of sense."

"What if you found me in possession of a trio of severed wolf heads?" I tried to sound sarcastic.

"Now that's more like what I've been orbiting around. Whatever killed those people, you took it out: But where's Valente fit? And why did you visit the Old Ways before they were killed? And when did the big, bad wolves learn to fire forty-five caliber bullets through a glass-packed silencer?" Salazar tapped the photo still in my hands. "That's what they dug out of his shoulder."

He sighed. "Mr. Fisher, I've made a career out of understanding the weird ones, but this mess is beyond me. Serial rapists, arsonists who get a sexual thrill from fire, men that are homicidally attracted to seven year old girls...I understand those cases. This...I suspect you're the only man on the planet who knows what really happened in Oklahoma."

"You might want to move."

I did so, a casual step to the right, just as a plump bumblebee dive-bombed over my shoulder. It crashed into Agent Salazar's stomach with an angry splat. My time with Veruca was paying off: I ducked for cover, before turning to look for the gunmen trying to kill me.

3

t wasn't hard to spot them. I had expected nothing, maybe a distant rooftop with a glint of metal on the edge. A man in a black suit, white shirt, and black tie, standing in the bed of a pickup truck was not what I had envisioned. With both hands, he held out an enormous pistol, the silenced barrel making it easily as long as a T-ball bat. Three more shots. The sickening whack of one told me it, too, hit Agent Salazar.

If I were a war wizard, I would've blown him up. My fireballs were unfortunately non-existent. I scrambled across the parking lot, taking shelter behind a forest green SUV. This did not deter my assailant as much as I had hoped. His gun didn't make a sound, but his bullets did as they screamed through the metal of the vehicle. Five shots hit in rapid succession. Two tore all the way through the vehicle, not far from my head. I needed a spell, or a bodyguard, more than ever. A distant cha-chunk suggested he was reloading.

I took a quick inventory: a fat wallet, a chaos pen knife, car keys, and a mace-spray-sized canister. I pulled the last item out, disabled the safety, and mumbled a luck spell over it. I dashed past the front end of the SUV and hurled my pocket flamethrower in the attacker's general direction. It landed with a clink in the bed of the pickup, but didn't ignite.

The man was reloading, but he wasn't alone. The driver and a passenger were crawling out of the cab. I couldn't see the driver well, but the passenger was pulling out an oversized gun of his own. I dove for cover, but didn't quite make it. A mini-pothole caught my foot and brought me crashing down to the asphalt. The passenger's first volley sailed overhead. The gunmen in the truck bed took a step to get a better angle. All the luck spells I'd ever thrown were finally catching up to me; karmic balance due on delivery.

My luck wasn't out. The gunman's step brought his foot down on the incendiary and the belch of flame enveloped both him and the passenger. Their screams were unpleasant.

The newly appeared wall of flame cut off the driver from view. I forced myself up off the ground and backpedaled into hiding behind the SUV. I drew my pen, but couldn't quite decide what I wanted it to look like. The chaos blade responded to my indecision with a cross between a short-sword and a katana with a main-gauche style blade catch near the hilt: I went with it.

The driver miscalculated that I had continued running forward, out of the lot. He moved up to where I had fallen, his back toward me as he scanned that direction, gun raised. I lunged and thrust a brilliant yellow pointy end into his jacket. There was a crackle as the blade pierced his flesh and tiny blue-white electrical arcs raced over the cloth. No blood came out, only a hiss of gray smoke. The man twitched like he had just shoved a fork into a wall outlet.

For a second, I thought I had stabbed a robot assassin. When I pulled out the chaos blade, though, his scream was human enough. Maybe it meant I was a bad person, but what I did next came naturally enough: I stabbed him again. The blade had changed to a murky gray hue. No wound ever appeared; the man's flesh turned to liquid as my swing advanced. By the time I checked my momentum, nothing was left of the assailant but a bubbling puddle and a few strips of cloth.

V had warned me about the "secondary" effects, but liquefying an enemy on contact seemed pretty damn primary to me.

4

Agent Salazar was down on the sidewalk, a pool of blood spreading out beneath him. I pulled out my grem-phone and dialed 911. The device sputtered, sparked, then fell to pieces in my hand. I cursed, but no sooner had the last modified toy car tire stopped rolling then I heard the sirens in the distance. Apparently, my deal with the Gremlin only covered three calls.

"Colin, we really need to go."

My dark voice was right.

"I usually am."

I stayed anyway. I had become associated with a lot of unpleasant things in recent weeks. I needed penance, even if only for psychological reasons. I grabbed Salazar's hand and squeezed it. "Come on, buddy, hang in there. The cavalry's on its way."

I thought he was unconscious, but his eyes opened and looked at me. "Thank you."

The next hour was a blur of names and faces. For all the officers, agents, paramedics, and special investigators I met, I don't really remember any of them. Unlike in my vagabond days, they all seemed to believe I was one of the good guys. They respected that I had stayed with the downed agent until help arrived…but they also respected my employer once his name came up. I answered their questions (sans any reference to magic or pocket flamethrowers), but they seemed more interested in running forensics on the scorched truck, two bodies, and the strange acidic slime puddle in the middle of the parking lot than in talking to me.

"Fisher." I recognized that voice immediately.

Her eyes were chestnut brown this time, not the lake water blue I'd seen in the Oklahoma interrogation room. A quick glimpse at her aura revealed no supernatural skin-riders. "Agent Devereaux."

She stood beside me and watched the technicians at work. "I told him coming to see you was a bad idea. I'll admit this wasn't exactly what I was worried about, but I knew it was a bad idea. Everything involving you is a bad idea."

I nodded, uncertain of what to say. I didn't know Rick Salazar well, but I had intuitively liked him. It didn't help that I had no idea what she did or didn't remember of our past conversation.

We stood there in silence. At last, she gave up and asked the question I'd been dreading for the last hour. "Were they trying to kill you or him?"

I went with my gut. "Me, I think."

"Yeah, me too." Her reply surprised me. "It'll be a tough sell. Most of the locals are already committed to calling it an attempted cop killing. Hard to blame them. I wouldn't want to investigate anything involving Valente International, either."

I didn't feel like talking. Agent Devereaux eventually continued. "Do you have it taken care of? Will Valente make sure the people responsible pay?"

I nodded. "If he doesn't, I will."

More silence followed before I asked, "What about Salazar? Is he going to make it?"

"Early reports, the docs think he has a chance. He caught

both shots in the belly, well away from heart and spine. Still ...."

"Still." I glanced around the crowded parking lot. "You want to go for a walk? My car's trapped inside the crime scene tape."

I could tell she wanted to remind me I was a suspected serial killer, but instead she nodded. "What's on your mind?"

I waited till we were comfortably away from the buzz of the crowd before answering. "I want to know what Salazar was looking for. I feel a little responsible for what happened to him."

"I was hoping you'd tell me. Whatever it was, he wasn't sharing with the rest of the team. Something about Oklahoma was gnawing at him...maybe in spite of, or more likely because of, the orders from on high to file the deaths under unsolved and move along."

"The Old Ways massacre and the animal-like bite marks. He showed me a few pictures, but that's as far as we got before the attack." That was what I started to say, before I dodged a silenced bullet via intuition, but that was way too weird, even for me to accept. How had I known it was coming? And why didn't I instinctively try to pull Salazar out of the way too?

"Yeah, that was the odd one. Three gunshot victims, fifty-seven heartless, frozen bodies. Our guy profiles as a lone killer, but there's no way one person did all that. It was almost like one of those religious cult suicides. But why that MO?" I could feel her eyes digging into me, as if the answers were written just beneath my skin.

"No, no, NO."

"Too late, I've made up my mind. It's penance and I'm doing it."

"Doesn't that have to be assigned by a priest or something?"

Before I could talk myself out of it, I opened my mouth. "Look, he seemed to think I knew what happened. I don't, at least not all of it, but if you send me his files on it, I'll see if I can't fill in the gaps. I think I can name the killer to you, maybe even prove it to your satisfaction, but I doubt it will be anything you can type up in a report."

She looked stunned. "Are you offering to turn state's evidence against Lucien Valente?"

"Not exactly. Just get me Salazar's file and I'll see what I can do." I was being a Good Samaritan, but I was also curious as to what exactly had happened at the Old Ways commune after Veruca and I had left. Thinking back on all the very young and very old living there, I could see how they would be easy pickings for an angry wendigo. But ....

"Why so many? Why didn't they run?"

"Exactly."

5

The dinner with the Unseelie ambassador that evening went a lot smoother than anticipated. I suspected that sending a less-than-brilliant troll as diplomat might have been an indirect commentary about the quality of Valente's previous personal wizards, but I didn't let that get in the way of having a good time. Of all my hospitality offerings, he took to the Kahlua with the greatest enthusiasm.

After the Eye of Winter, the troll was almost mundane by comparison. If you squinted just right, he looked human...if NFL defensive linemen counted as human. His skin looked professionally tanned, every ravenesque hair was gelled in place, and his hunter green suit was perfectly tailored to his massive frame. His physical form was easily three inches taller than mine, but over it all hung the shadow of his true self. The troll's essence was so strong that no attempt to disguise him as human could ever be wholly successful. Still, I appreciated the attempt at camouflage—his size was unnerving even without his true form.

He spoke in between massive gulps of coffee liquor. "I tell you, wiz. You sure know how to throw dinner. Though ...." He leaned closer. "You don't know much about negotiating.

Number one rule: let the troll have what he wants."

It came out more like nee-goat-shheat, which was a comfort to me. Despite his massive size, he was sloshed drunk, one step removed from stuporville.

"Remind me why that's a good thing? I don't want to be the one to bounce this guy after last call."

The laws of hospitality forbade physical violence during this meeting for about fifteen different reasons. No, if he was really drunk, it meant I didn't have to worry about him tricking me.

"But he's dumb as a box of...yeah, that would be pretty embarrassing."

"Sir Kerath, I appreciate the free advice, but my instructions were unequivocal: I cannot sell that tract of land to the court." I paused to pour a quarter-inch in my glass, before emptying the rest of the bottle in Kerath's. "But ...."

"But what?" The troll's voice could have been heard on the other side of my massive laboratory residence. Next to him, it was deafening.

I did my best to politely ignore the ringing in my ears and settled back into my chair. "No, no. I should not have said anything."

"Tell me. Kerath commands it."

I'm guessing that's what he said. Whatever the fae usually drank, I don't think it was processed via modern distillation technology. "I shouldn't...but since you wish it, Sir Kerath, I will. Perhaps if I knew what your people needed the land for, I could present a suitable counteroffer."

Kerath shook his head, like a large dog trying to shed water. "What little...I mean, what wiz say?"

"What do the Unseelie intend to do with the land?"

"Oh," he said, sitting up in his chair. "Need it for crossing over."

I nodded sagaciously. Despite spending much of my free time with Veruca, I had not been idle in my weeks with Valente International. The land in question was a barren strip of tundra in

Northern Canada. From the Valente standpoint, the problem was underground: there was a significant natural gas deposit. Mystically, a pair of ley lines intersected there, above ground, and I had suspected they had something to do with the Unseelie's interest. Crossing over was a new term to me, but by the context I assumed they meant they could use it to move things from the fairy world to here and vice versa. I translated that into a guess. "Bringing in or shipping out?"

"Out. Spot not very good for in. But be right for out in a couple of weeks." He suddenly stopped and slapped himself on the forehead. "Me not supposed to tell you that."

I shook my head slowly. "I won't mention it, Sir Kerath. How long will it be usable?"

The troll paused uncertain. He drained his glass, then spoke. "Two weeks. New moon to full moon."

"What if Valente offered to loan the area to the court for those two weeks?"

Kerath mulled it over, his lubricated gears grinding very slowly now. "How much?"

For the land outright, he had brought five hundred thousand dollars, but Kerath had hinted that other barter might be available. The money to be gained here was irrelevant. Lucien had money; he wanted power and influence. "Nothing is to be taken from the land or under the land. Possession transfers to the Unseelie Court from the start of the new moon until the last night of the corresponding full moon. Assuming these conditions, Valente International will satisfy itself with fifteen days obedient service, from a named Unseelie of our choosing, on the days of our choosing, as specified in the ancient covenants regarding bonds of service. You get our land for fifteen days…we get one of the fae for fifteen days."

That shook him. He leaned back and appeared to instantly sober. "I should be more careful, wizard. You are not as mentally deficient as Valente's reputation would suggest." Kerath paused.

"Perhaps we should start our negotiations again, sans theatrics."

Now it was my turn to look shocked.

6

It was well past midnight before Kerath and I hammered out a lease acceptable to both sides. Once we each accepted the other wasn't as dumb as he looked, we found each other's company far more enjoyable. Kerath had been chosen as ambassador because he had attended law school at Ohio State. The only part true to stereotype was that it had been paid for by football scholarship. As it turned out, he could suppress most of his fae aura when he wanted to.

"The rental agreement will not thrill the court, I'm afraid," Kerath confessed. "They had hoped to realize a financial gain, while simultaneously gaining access to the site for the crossing over.

"But the deal is fair," I insisted, as I walked him to the door.

"That it is, Wizard Fisher," he acknowledged. "But if my queen wanted fair deals, she wouldn't have sent me to law school."

I started to open the front door, then stopped. "My predecessors...they really would have sold that land for a measly half-mill? You're not that scary looking."

"Maybe, maybe not." Kerath laughed. "They might not have

sold it. But they would have neglected the part about not taking anything on, or under, the land in the rental agreement. And they would have asked for cash, not favors or service."

We walked quietly into the chill Boston night. I had been inside preparing dinner when Kerath arrived and was curious to see what kind of transportation Ohio State educated troll lawyers used in the mortal realm. I don't know what I expected, but a cherry red Fiat convertible was not it. I did a double-take as he stepped next to it.

Kerath blushed. "The ladies like it...and I usually keep the top down."

"I think you'd have to."

He shrugged. "Size only matters if you let it." Kerath did a double-take over my shoulder. "Did you tell anyone about our meeting?"

"Only those in the company relevant to the topic. Why?"

He grunted. "Five hundred yards behind you. Government issued vehicle. Her eyes are drilling holes into both of us."

I glanced behind me, but couldn't make out anything beyond the vague shade of a sedan. "How can you tell?"

"Don't let the handsome exterior fool you. I'm still a troll; night time is our time."

I desperately wanted to play casual, which is always the easiest way to feel awkward and tense. "A spy?"

"Could be. The Seelie are bound to be interested." Kerath scratched his chin for a moment, before walking past me. "Only one way to find out."

Matching step for step with a purposefully moving troll was impossible. He closed on the car in a matter of seconds. The dome light clicked on as the driver's door opened. Whoever was inside had decided they didn't want to be sitting down when Kerath arrived. For the second time in twenty-four hours, my hand was unconsciously groping about for the handle of my chaos blade.

"Hold it right there, big guy. Federal agent." Agent Devereaux displayed her gold shield as if it were a cross of faith and Kerath was a marauding vampire.

I jogged to catch up. "It's all right, Kerath. She's a friend...right?" I looked at her for reassurance.

She just kept eyeing the troll nervously. He was actively suppressing his trollishness, but he was still mammothly intimidating. At last, Devereaux said, "Yeah, a friend. I just came by to let you know about Salazar's condition."

Kerath offered her a small bow. "My apologies, then. I did not mean to frighten you. Mr. Fisher and I have been engaged in some rather important business negotiations all evening."

"Business negotiations?" She shook her head. "No, no, I'm off duty. I don't want to know."

I resented the implications that my business was, by definition, criminal. "Hey, it's not like that. We were just …."

"Shut up and run."

"What?"

"No questions, just run."

I grabbed Devereaux's arm and pulled her out of the way, just as my mind registered the rumble of the engine. A large black van burst out of the night, barreling straight down on us. Devereaux resisted, the momentum clash throwing us both down to the ground, dead center of the van's path. Rather than swerve away, the van accelerated. Its chrome bumper glimmered with the promise of death.

I really wished I knew how to throw a fireball.

7

There was a loud metallic shriek of impact, but no pain. The van slammed to a stop three feet from my face. In a matter of seconds, Kerath had grown a foot taller and two feet wider. The front end of the vehicle collapsed against his oversized ham-hock fists. The van's momentum stopped completely, but the troll didn't even budge.

"What the hell? I knew all those luck ...."

Before I could finish my sentence, Devereaux was yanking me up to my feet. My shoulder, still tender from my last dance with the wendigo, protested. "Run," she said, echoing my subconscious.

My feet obeyed, though I didn't understand. My hearing was ripped away by a massive explosion. After sound left, my connection to Earth was broken: the force of the blast flung me ragdoll style. For a moment, I hurtled effortlessly through space, before a sudden and harsh reintroduction to the ground.

I wanted to pass out, rather than feel the pain, but my body refused to cooperate. Instead, I lay there wishing the ringing would leave my ears alone. When it had died down to a loud roar, I rolled over to find Devereaux. "You okay?"

She nodded a little, but didn't try to stand up.

"Thanks…how did you know it would blow?"

With effort, she forced herself to sit up. "Explosives wired to the undercarriage. Got a pretty good look at them after you tripped me." Devereaux grunted as her hands explored her ribs. "Are people always trying to kill you or is it just when you're within shouting distance of an FBI agent?"

I shook my head gingerly, still not wanting to stand. "Just feds and faeries, I guess…oh crap." I forced myself to stand then, as I remembered Sir Kerath. His body lay fifty feet off, full troll now. What little of his clothing hadn't been torn apart by the sudden growth had been burnt off by the blast.

I rushed over to him and knelt, feeling for a pulse. Mercifully, troll wrist anatomy was not vastly different and I soon found his weak, but present, heartbeat. I heard Devereaux's footsteps behind me. "What on Earth …" Her voice trailed off.

"Troll," I answered. "Unseelie Court ambassador, he just saved our lives, and I don't have time to explain right now." I patted Kerath's cheek. "Kerath, come on, wake up. I don't know what to do here."

His wounds were extensive. He may have stopped the runaway vehicle with little effort, but the fiery explosion had caught him at ground zero. I heard Devereaux behind me, pushing buttons on what I could only pray wasn't a cellphone."

I glanced back, saw that it was, and yelled, "Devereaux! Put that damn thing down and help me get him back inside…or do you want to explain to the Boston PD what a troll is?"

That caught her and she pulled the phone down from her face. "But I don't even know what a troll is."

"My point exactly. Now help me get him inside and I'll explain it to you. Leave him out here and you can handle explanations to all the first responders."

"But they'd want to talk to you…you'd have to explain," she stammered.

I grinned. "Can't talk to a Valente employee without a warrant."

Her look was thunderous, but she bent over and hooked her arms under Kerath's knees.

8

etting Kerath back upstairs and inside my apartment was rough work, but Agent Devereaux, despite her petite frame, was in much better shape than I was. I cleared the dinner table with a dish-scattering back arm sweep and laid him on top of it, just as the first sirens pulled into the parking lot.

Devereaux was frantic. "What do I tell them?"

I looked over Kerath's wounds. I remembered stories of trollish regeneration, but his had only stabilized, not improved. I had to hope whatever vital force let him go toe to toe with a van would hold him a little longer. "Stick to the facts. A van charged us, tried to run us down, then it blew up." I paused for a second. "Do we have to tell them anything?"

"I'm a federal agent, Fisher. I can't just hide behind a Valente lawyer."

I wanted to call Duchess right then, but I had no desire to explain to my boss why an FBI agent was making midnight house calls any more than Devereaux wanted to explain what a troll was. "Look, just tell them what you have to and keep them out of here. I've got to do something to save him."

"Right." She nodded, as if battlefield triage was an everyday thing. "But you owe me an explanation." With that, she disappeared, closing the front door behind her.

Turning back to Kerath, I wondered what would happen if I let an Unseelie Ambassador die during a diplomatic meeting. I was certain the fae would want reparations far more dire than a single mortal child or a hundred years of slave labor. Again, I frantically whispered in the troll's ear, "Sir Kerath, if you can hear me, I really need you to pull through this."

His voice was raspy, as scorched as his skin. "Fairy .... Get to...fairy ring."

It made sense. He needed to get home. In the safety of Fairy, he could heal...but how? I wasn't intimately familiar with any fairy rings in the area...or in the real world, period. Certainly, I believed such things existed, but ....

"Quit thinking, start wizarding."

"For once, you're right."

"How about twice? Who told you to run?"

"Okay, so what do I do?" I wondered.

"Get him back to Fairyland. If he dies there, it's not on us."

"And it might help heal him, too, right?"

"Sure...as if that were the important issue."

I made a whirlwind tour of the lab, scooping up everything I could that I even vaguely thought would help. I had the permanent silver circle, but there was zero chance of me being able to get Kerath from my table to the circle without help. If a circle was needed, it would have to come to him. I grabbed a bag of sugar from the kitchen, tore open its top corner, and began pouring it in a clockwise ring around the dining table. It wasn't a perfect circle, but it would have to do.

I stepped in and deposited my tools on one of the chairs. I noticed, with dismay, that I'd forgotten my athame.

"Whoa, whoa, shouldn't we have a plan here?"

"You were the one who said to start wizarding. It's a little late to pull back now."

"I meant 'grab the Necronomicon and find a spell', not 'start slinging magic helter-skelter.'"

"No Necronomicon needed. I can do this. I'm a professional wizard, remember?"

I pulled the chaos blade from my pocket and willed it into the shape of a ritual dagger. From the inside of the circle, I paced the sugar ring, holding the blade tip over the circle, trying to visualize the whole process in my mind.

I felt the circle snap shut, sealing the magical energies inside with me and Kerath. I placed a half-eaten chocolate bar on his chest and laid both massive hands on top of it, one at a time. The wrapper stuck out from underneath like a lily in the grasp of a sleeping Snow White from a very fractured fairy tale. Hopefully, I wouldn't have to kiss Kerath to save him.

I knelt into genuflection, still uncertain what I needed to do. I briefly prayed first, "God, I haven't always been the best Catholic, but I could really use a little divine guidance right now. Help me know the right words to use."

"And let's be honest: YOU owe their kind for the whole Inquisition thing."

I found myself humming a few bars from an old Mel Brooks movie, stopped myself in horror when I realized what it was, then started again as a plan began to hatch in my addled brain. The Inquisition had undoubtedly wiped out hundreds of fae living in mortal disguise, forced them back into Fairy, even as it had forced many Jewish families into hiding or conversion. But a little Jewish humor might just do the trick...I would just have to improvise a few lines at the end. I tried to picture Mel Brooks dressed as the Inquisitor Torquemada before breaking into full out song.

"The Inquisition, what a show!

The Inquisition, here we go!

The Inquisition, watch 'em go!

We're the Inquisition and we're here to stay.

Oh, the Inquisition's here and we're here to stay!
Oh, the Inquisition's here, but you're not here to stay!
Oh, the Inquisition's here, but you're not here to stay!
Oh, the Inquisition's here, but you're not here to stay!"

I belted it out at full volume, including a dance number that I am glad there were no conscious witnesses of. If no one saw me doing chorus girl kicks, I could retain my wizardly dignity. I could feel the energy growing with each line and by the time I stopped singing, the air was thick with power...but Kerath was still lying on the table. My inner voice may have been right about needing a plan before starting to use magic at random, but I was trapped now.

As I breathed in the crackling, energetic air, I recalled that initial image of Mel Brooks as Torquemada. I tried to breathe that in, to let the Torquemada persona cover me, visualizing myself as the Spanish Grand Inquisitor. In my most solemn voice, I intoned, "Sir Kerath, by order of the Grand Inquisition, you are hereby banished to the Fairy realm for a term of no less than one day!" I slashed out behind me with the chaos blade, breaking the flow of the circle, visualizing it as a judge's gavel banging down.

Something did bang down, with a knock-knock. The power rushed out of the circle, the rustling air momentarily blinding me. When I could see again, Kerath was gone...along with my dining table. The knock-knock came again and this time I placed it as coming from my front door.

9

I thought of putting myself back together before answering, but decided the disheveled, traumatized look might help increase the believability of my story. I reshaped the chaos blade, put it away, and grabbed an empty red wine bottle from the kitchen for prop use. I opened up my front door, expecting to see an apologetic Devereaux and a half-dozen angry police investigators. Instead, the swinging door revealed just Agent Devereaux.

She stepped past me into the apartment, pushing the door closed as she passed. "All right, I think that's taken care of. I need to stop being around you; I'm getting spoiled by how efficient your boss's name is. They suddenly decided it would be easier to tell the media that someone wants to blow up a bunch of housing for sex offenders than to...wait, where's the troll?"

"Back in Fairy, I hope."

She shook her head like a dog with a chew toy. "No, no, I mean, where is he? Like a secret panel or a closet or ....."

I slid one of my now-table-less chairs towards her, motioned for her to sit, and went towards the kitchen. "He's gone. I cast a spell and opened up a portal back to Fairyland for him. You can either sit down, accept that, and I'll try to explain in more detail."

I rummaged around for a pair of glasses, then pulled a gallon of milk from the fridge. "Or you can reject that as the ramblings of a crazy man and nothing I can say will help you make any sense of this."

When I came back into the main room, she was indeed seated. I handed her a glass of milk and pulled up a chair opposite her. I sat down and waited for her to say something, anything. After a long minute, she gave a harsh nod, wordlessly telling me to go on.

"Anything you repeat outside this room will likely earn you a trip to the loony bin, but I assure you it's the truth. I am Lucien Valente's personal wizard. He hired me to deal with the thing that was eating his employees back in Oklahoma. He liked my work, so he's kept me around." I took a sip of my milk and was pleased to see she did the same. "Does that fit? Can you wrap your mind around the idea of corporate wizards?"

"Wizard? And not as a euphemism for problem solver, creative acquisitions, or assassin?"

I almost snarked that no, that would be my girlfriend, but decided some details were better left out. "Wizard as in Merlin-stuff...magic, plain and simple magic." She was dazed and confused, wanting to believe, but not quite there. I pointed across the room. "See that case? Those jewels belonged to a nineteenth century spiritualist, who claimed they were the key to the success of her séances. Those spears over there are replicas of the one that pierced the side of Christ, made by the Nazis. The prayer rugs hanging on the back wall are all a way of disguising old teachings during the spread of Islam: the craftsmen hid names of djinns and the basic instructions on how to summon them within the weave of the fabric. You think Valente would drop big bucks on all the stuff unless he was absolutely certain that there was something to it?"

Devereaux's eyes slowly snaked around the rest of the apartment, seeing for the first time all the other display cases I hadn't mentioned and row upon row of bookshelves. "What is this place?"

"My home...and my lab." I paused. "Stay with me, Agent. I need to make sure you understand exactly what you're dealing with."

"Magic. Got it," she mumbled. "Like men who turn into trolls and can stop speeding vans with their bare hands."

"Not exactly. Kerath was born a troll, but he can disguise himself as a man. I was born a man ..."

"Ate an old girlfriend to get some power."

"... and learned how to use magic." I was at a loss for how to proceed. Normally this was the part where I would downplay my skill and pretend like I couldn't do anything more impressive than a birthday party trick. The vanished dining table and missing troll said otherwise. In the back of my mind, I thought it couldn't hurt to let an FBI agent think I was a tad more powerful than I actually was.

She slowly recovered from the shock of it all, the color returning to her cheeks. "So you and the troll were discussing company business, Valente business, tonight? And somebody tried to run you over with a backup plan of blowing you up. No driver, police are thinking robotic device...but it could've been magic, couldn't it? A magic assassin van?"

I nodded. Based on what I had seen this afternoon at the ATM, I suspected it was a little more mundane than that, but it didn't matter. At the heart of it, magic was a technology, same as robotics. The only difference was that people had forgotten how to use one of them, even as they were excelling at refining the other. I was about to say something when my brain snagged on something funny. For the first day in over a month, I was without the benefit of my demon-spawn bodyguard...and somebody had tried to kill me twice since she'd left. I shuddered and downed the rest of my milk in one shot.

"And the slime in the parking lot this afternoon? Did they try to attack you with some kind of acid golem or ...."

I cut her off. "Actually, that was me. There were three assailants. The puddle was what I did to one of them."

"And it wasn't a stray bullet that just happened to hit their gas tank, either, was it?"

"Guilty as charged, though I had a little technological assist there."

She sat straight up in her chair and handed me her glass. "All right, Mr. Fisher. I'm ready to hear what really happened in Oklahoma. And I could probably use a glass of something stronger than milk."

10

"**S**o this wendigo thing was some kind of ancient beast and the Old Ways shaman had managed to whip it up into a murderous frenzy?" Andrea Devereaux shook her head slowly. "You know, I think the hardest part for me to believe is that Valente's company played the part of the hero in killing the wendigoes off."

She was catching on quicker than I had at first. "See what I mean about telling you the truth, but not giving you anything you can type up for a report? I've held the stuffed and mounted heads of all three wendigoes and it still feels unreal to me at times."

"I think the bureau is just glad it's over: 61 bodies in Oklahoma, 1 in Joplin, and 2 in Saint Louis. That's a heck of a body count to just sweep under the rug, but they're doing it. They don't know anything about wendigoes and wouldn't believe me if I told them…but they know it's not natural, either. Official word says it's over, so it's over."

The night was drawing closer to morning and I had consumed more than my fair share of alcohol since the sun had set, but my mind wasn't that dull yet. Still, I didn't want to alarm her if I didn't have to. "Did you bring Salazar's file with you? I would like to take a look at it if I could." I fumbled for a plausible excuse. "Maybe he came up with something on the Old Ways I missed, some background on what pushed the old woman over the edge."

I don't think she bought it entirely, but she stood up anyway. "Yeah, it's out in my car. I'll go grab it."

After I let her out, I tried not to process any of the extras. They were words not easily unheard, though: one in Joplin, two in Saint Louis. Had those happened before we killed them? Maybe the wendigo had woken up there and used those as stopovers to get breakfast en route to its destination in Oklahoma. But, either way, why hadn't I heard about them?

"Because they weren't Valente employees."

That fit. I knew about all the attacks on people who fell under the corporate umbrella of Valente International. The Old Ways massacre and these three took me by surprise, because they weren't under Valente's protection. I remembered something from my discussion with the Eye of Winter about two separate events: a man walking the Shadowlands *and* the woman calling down the curse. Was there an uncursed wendigo, woken by the shadow walker, out there? And if so, was it my responsibility to stop it? I wasn't walking the Shadowlands and I sure wasn't being paid to protect the public, but somehow I felt vaguely responsible. It wasn't that I had caused it...but I knew I had the power to stop it and with that power...Agent Devereaux's return knock broke my reverie.

11

I would pay a lot to know what Andrea Devereaux, special agent, Behavioral Sciences Investigative, was thinking as she watched me flip through the pages of the dog-eared file. I tried my best to be nonchalant, as if I expected and understood everything that was between its manila covers, while secretly memorizing every line. I checked and re-checked names and dates, trying to fix the timeline in my own mind, lining up my whereabouts for each. I would have liked a few hours alone with the file, but instead I settled for a few minutes.

I closed it up and offered it to her. "It all fits. Definitely a wendigo pack."

"And they're all dead?" I couldn't tell if she was eyeing me with suspicion or if it was residual fear of the things that go bump, growl, and bite in the night.

I had been right on one thing: I hadn't heard about the other three killings, because despite the same M.O., the victims weren't Valente employees, ergo, no company interest. I had been wrong, however, about the direction and timing of the Joplin and Saint Louis killings. I was theorizing without facts; now I had facts, no matter how much I disliked them. I lied to her. "Three, bagged and tagged."

"How is it a lie? We killed three."

"It's a lie in that it makes no mention of a fourth."

I watched her to see if she would buy it. She seemed to. Maybe she didn't, but it was well past two in the morning and all of her novel experience circuits had been overloaded in the last few hours, so she nodded. "Good. Not a lot I can use, but it's good to know, I suppose."

"That's what I keep telling myself. It's nice to know how far down the rabbit hole goes, even if what lives at the end of it scares the bejeezus out of me." I tried to sound friendly, while secretly wishing she'd decide it was time to leave and never come back.

She yawned. "I should probably call it a night." She paused. "Look, Colin, if you ever need anything...y'know, stuff like this." Her silence was longer this time, her voice nearly inaudible when she finished, "Or help getting away from Valente, just let me know."

I nodded sagaciously, but said nothing. She favored me with one last smile, which drove home the reminder of just how much she looked like long-lost Sarai, then turned and reached for the door knob. I hoped she stayed the hell away from me, but not because I disliked her. I was starting to take a shine to her and the world always need more people like Sarai. But I was absolutely certain being around me was a really good way to die.

Before going to bed, I walked downstairs to use the payphone in the parking lot. I left a detailed message with Duchess of what I needed, then trudged back upstairs. My hand never left the grip of my chaos blade, but if there were any assassins waiting in the wings, no one tried anything. I crashed into a deep sleep, where my thoughts roamed through ancient forests full of trolls struggling for their next breath.

12

T he next week was a blur to me. Between settling in, the side projects I was working on, waiting for word that the fae courts had decided to go to war with Valente International, and brushing up on how to make a Thanksgiving dinner, I barely had time to stop and breathe. Veruca stayed gone longer than I had expected, which helped me get half the time I needed, but I missed her fiercely. She had gotten under my skin in a way no one since Sarai had, but I hadn't realized just how deep until she was gone.

It was late Thursday afternoon, with a turkey far too large for me already roasting in the oven, when I heard the lock on the front door tumbling. By the time I escaped the kitchen, Veruca was already relocking it behind her. I disengaged from my apron and oven mitt before assaulting her with a hug.

My right hand came back sticky and wet, a dark crimson under the pale afternoon sun of the western window. Veruca shook her one long bang, today a somber gray, then pulled me back into the hug.

I tried to revel in it, before saying, "Not your blood, I hope."

"Nope." I waited for more details, but none were

forthcoming. Instead, after a long, intense hug, she sniffed the air and commented, "It actually smells like Thanksgiving in here."

"And now that you're back, I have something to be thankful for." I gently kissed her cold lips.

It came out so sickeningly sweet I half-expected her to body slam me for it. Veruca was a lot of things, but sentimental wasn't one of them. Instead, she surprised me by kissing me back. "Think dinner will be ready by the time I get out of the shower?"

I grinned. "Only if I stay in the kitchen and cook."

V patted my back as she pulled away. "Well then, get your cook on. I'm starving." She paused, then turned back to kiss me again. "And I missed you." That said, she disappeared into the bathroom.

I washed the blood off my hand and arm, then turned my attention to a rather stubborn pot of mashed potatoes. I silently turned the pieces of the mystery that was Veruca over in my mind, but didn't come up with anything satisfactory. The blood from an international killing would have long since dried or removed. I didn't know much about Veruca's work, but I doubted that she liked getting her hands dirty if she didn't have to. That suggested she had killed someone locally and that she hadn't planned the killing ahead of time. I had reasoned it that far, and no further, when I heard a thunderous knock at the front door.

My apron was still off from before, but this time I had to disengage my bloody shirt. A topless chef was strange, but not illegal. I checked my pants pocket to make sure the chaos blade was still in there, before unlocking the dead bolt.

Kerath, fully dressed and far healthier than when last I'd seen him, cocked an eyebrow at me. "I didn't know Thanksgiving was that kind of party in Boston. In Ohio, we saved *au natural* for New Years and Super Bowl Sunday."

I didn't know if it was appropriate diplomatic protocol, but I hugged him, too. "Glad to see you made it. You had me more than a little worried."

"Made it?" A voice queried from beside him. "I thought you said we weren't expected."

It took an effort to look around Kerath's massive frame to see the petite blond beside him. She was pretty, but too thin, with all her facial features at sharp angles. "No, I mean, I'm surprised he's alive. Last time I saw him ...." I paused unsure how much she knew or was prudent to say.

Kerath blushed a slight green. "Ah, it'd take a lot more than one little van to kill me. Wizard Fisher, this is my betrothed. Lady Selena, this is the wizard who fought beside me."

I had stepped back inside the apartment and couldn't see her when she spoke. "For which we are both grateful, Wizard. My beloved tells me this is the appropriate day in your world for expressing thanks."

I hoped this wasn't going the direction of some stories I had read. I liked Kerath, but I didn't need him as a constant companion until he found a way to save my life. "Well, Sir Kerath helped me as much as I helped him." The smell of something burning distracted me. "Do you two want to come on in? I'm in the middle of cooking dinner."

I hurried back into the kitchen as the scent of smoke grew stronger. It took me a half hour of frantic effort to save what I could of the meal. In the end, our Thanksgiving dinner consisted of a slightly dry turkey, reasonably decent sweet potatoes, and a trio of pizzas. I called out for the last item after I pronounced the mashed potatoes and cranberry sauce dead on arrival.

13

The meal went peaceably enough. I had set up a card table where my dining table used to be, before I knew about the extra guests. When I had the cooking under control, I poked my head out of the kitchen long enough to discover the card table had been replaced. In its place was a massive, round table that looked like it had been carved from a solid block of ice. The chairs were dark green, save for where a pair of pale purple rose blooms crowned the top of each chair. Seven of them in all, looking more grown than made, surrounded the table.

Veruca broke off her conversation with Selena to shoot me a curious glance. "Interesting company you keep when I'm away."

I shrugged and went back to finish the meal. The table occupied my mind, as I wondered how the two fae had gotten it in there without me feeling even the hint of magic.

"Do not meddle in the affairs of Fairy, for you are mortal and easily duped? Relax, I can take 'em if it comes to that."

Fortunately, Selena barely ate, so the meal fit for an army managed to find Veruca, Kerath, and me. I hoped her eating habits weren't a reflection of my cooking. I'll admit it wasn't great, but it wasn't bad, either.

After dinner, Selena formally presented the table to me, in replacement of one that I had lost while saving her love, Kerath. I graciously accepted, while being careful to point out that neither of us owed the other anything in way of gifts or boons. Veruca asked what had happened to the old one. Kerath responded in the way that only a great trial lawyer could, recounting our tight negotiations and the mysterious ambush afterward with a flair for dramatic storytelling. He seemed to relish the drama in every detail, though I noticed he left Agent Devereaux out of the story.

Veruca's expression was grim as he finished. "You're becoming popular, Colin. There was another one waiting for you when I came home today."

I thought back to the blood. "Looks that way. Three guys tried earlier the same day as the exploding van."

"Three?" she asked, her look more proud than surprised, as if our training together was paying off.

"Three. Big guns, bigger silencers."

Kerath leaned forward on to the table. "Yes. The Faceless Ones can be quite relentless."

Veruca was verbally faster than me on the reply. "Faceless Ones?" I was going to say the same, though somewhere in my soul that phrase already echoed around.

Selena cleared her throat. "A secret organization of humans bent on ruling the mortal world. Our queen is most unhappy that they attacked her emissary. She sends word that her resources are at your disposal in seeking revenge against them, Wizard Fisher."

I digested that over an already-full belly of turkey and pizza. At last, I said, "Tell Hher Majesty thank you for me."

Veruca gulped the last of her wine. "But what do they want with Colin?"

All three of them looked at me. I simply shrugged. "Not a clue."

"Really? I thought you were smarter than that."

14

That night, I tossed and turned in my sleep. It was good to have Veruca back in bed with me, but even her presence couldn't pry me free from the thoughts than ran untamed through my mind. Weather reports, unexpected FBI visitors, secret societies, both ancient and modern, all darted haphazardly through my consciousness.

Around one AM, I gave up on sleep and went out into the main room, I listened to the national weather service while meditating in the middle of my circle. Pittsburgh was being blanketed by a turkey day blizzard. I made a mental note to have Veruca check the missing person reports Monday. The distances between Oklahoma City, Tulsa, Joplin, Saint Louis, Memphis, Nashville, and Pittsburgh were sorted, analyzed, then re-sorted. I tried to remember if that was the route Veruca and I had driven in Dora, but found my memories badly entangled with my nightmares and personal suspicions. Still, if I was making this up, how had I known a storm would hit Pennsylvania this weekend?

"Yeah, but you predicted Philadelphia, not Pittsburgh," my dark voice noted.

"I was wondering when you would show up."

"Your thoughts seemed plenty dark and desperate without any help from me."

"I did expect Philly. Makes me wonder if I'm wrong …."

"Or if it's speeding up."

"Something like that. There won't be any bodies this time. It's getting smarter, covering its tracks."

"If there's another wendigo out there. It could just be a copycat. There's some really sick people out there."

"What about the missing people in Memphis and Nashville?"

"Plenty of unexplained missing in every major city. Again, there's some really sick people out there."

"And the weather patterns?"

"It's late November, Colin. Snow happens."

I paused and worked on clearing the clutter from my head. Deep breath in, deep breath out. I counted backward from 33 before turning to the next topic. Where had I heard of the Faceless before?

"The Eye of Winter. Something about faceless men who had trained the wendigoes in ancient times."

"Is that the connection? Are one of these people the shadowwalker?"

The lack of response scared me. Did the monster living inside of me not know the answer? Or worse still, did it know, but was too afraid to tell?

Even in a deep trance, I nearly jumped out of my skin when Veruca slid an arm around my shoulders. "You okay, Colin?"

The concern in her voice was touching. I just wished I knew the answer to her question.

15

L ucien Valente invited me to breakfast the next week. I dressed to the standards of a country club, as best I could, but the address he gave me turned out to be an IHOP. This time, we were both the best dressed men to ever grace a discount pancake joint. As before, he insisted that I eat a little off of his plate before ordering anything for myself.

"Why pancakes?" I asked.

Lucien grinned. "Who would think to look for the two of us here? Unpredictable targets are hard to assassinate."

I added an extra creamer to my coffee. "I take it Veruca has been talking."

"I take attempts on the lives of my employees seriously." He took a sip of his coffee. "Anything I need to do to make the assassins go away?"

"You know anything about a group called the Faceless Men or why they wouldn't want you to have a personal wizard?"

He paused to allow the waiter to deliver my food and refresh our carafe. "No. I'm aware of numerous cabals, would-be Illuminati…but none by that name and none that have expressed an interest in my previous wizards."

I considered mentioning the possible connection to the wendigoes before deciding against it. Maybe it was the way Dorothy had died, but I thought of that business as personal. "It's possible the fae invented them or are trying to trick us into doing their dirty work for them. Both times I've heard of them, it's been off of a fairy's lips."

Lucien replied, but whatever he said, I didn't hear it. I suddenly realized my last statement wasn't entirely true. I had heard of the Faceless before, from my own lips. True, it hadn't been my voice, but I'd been the one speaking. I could feel my dark subconscious probing around the edges of the new revelation and instinctively shut him out from what I was thinking.

When Valente finished speaking, I nodded sagaciously, as if I had been hanging on his every word. I tried to be polite, useful, and knowledgeable throughout the rest of the meal, but my thoughts were busy elsewhere.

16

It wasn't until the third of December that my opportunity came. Veruca got a call from Lucien that afternoon and left with one of those excuses that meant I didn't want to know where she was going to be for the next five or six hours. Normally, it might have bothered me that my girlfriend was going off to kill someone. Today, I just hoped it meant I could finally do some killing of my own.

As soon as she was gone, I made a hurried tour of the apartment to load up my duffel bag: three black candles, a lighter, one of the spear replicas, the Necronomicon, and enough snacks to keep my belly quiet through a weekend camping trip.

When I was satisfied that I had what I needed, I called Duchess Deluce.

"Valente International."

"Duchess, it's Fisher. I need a favor."

She paused for a moment. "What can I do for you, Mr. Fisher?"

"There's a rest stop on I-90 about 20 miles west of Boston." I checked the mile marker again before relaying it. "I need it closed down 'til sunrise. Access for me and my car only."

"Contrary to popular belief, I don't control the state government, Mr. Fisher. What should I tell the Department of Transportation to accomplish that feat?"

I had to think for a moment. I had assumed Miss Deluce could accomplish it effortlessly. "Chemical leak. Tell them I'm the company inspector." I paused. "Whatever bribe it takes to get them to keep quiet about it, take it out of my next paycheck."

"Mr. Valente always insists on paying expenses. This is company business, right?"

I hesitated. It was business, but that didn't mean I wanted to share what I was up to. If I was right, I didn't want to tell anyone, ever, under any conditions. "Just checking a lead on the Faceless," I lied.

"I don't need to know details, Mr. Fisher," Duchess chided. "The boss has made it quite clear you report to him and him alone." I could hear computer keys typing in the background. "In your orientation packet, I gave you two extra employee IDs, Mr. Fisher. One of them is in the name of Richard Dugger. Take that one with you and if anyone asks you for identification, give them that. The rest stop will be all yours 'til noon tomorrow."

I thanked her, hung up, and fished out the card she had mentioned. The only thing left to do was to decide whether this was really a good idea or not. If I was smart, I would wait until Veruca came home, tell her everything, and go tackle this together. The truth was, I was more afraid of what might happen to her than I was of what might happen to me. I still remembered that prophetic insight when I first looked into her eyes. I would give anything, even my own life, not to be the cause of her death.

I brewed one last cup of coffee to give Duchess time to work out the details, then headed out the door before I could talk myself out of it. The roads out of Boston were strangely deserted that day as Dora and I muscled our way out of town. It was as if the entire city could sense the coming showdown.

The empty roads let me mull things over, putting together

again the pieces I had already linked in the past week. It had been a long year for me. I had rung in the New Year just outside of Seattle, worked my way down the West Coast through January and February. In March, I had driven across the southwest, heading east. I had stopped in Oklahoma City in mid-March before heading down to New Orleans. I wondered if I had slept that night and, if I did, what I had dreamt about.

I would have been working at a bar back in the Big Easy when the old woman wrote her curse in April. I understood now where I had gone wrong in the investigation: I had assumed that people's actions were what mattered. My wrong assumption led to my equally wrong belief that the old woman had called the wendigo. The Eye of Winter knew better: the wendigo had called to the old woman, nurturing her hate, prompting her to free it with her curse. While I was bouncing around the South, playing a renaissance fair wizard or working at the docks, Hungry Winter was gathering its strength and nursing its pups.

With wendigoes as the caller, rather than the called, it was easy to understand what it did after it was killed: it called again. The old woman may have been dead, but there must have been another in the Old Ways with a spiritual sensitivity. How had the deal been phrased? Give me your lives, your energy, your heart, and I will give you vengeance. It had been something like that. The people didn't run, didn't scatter from the wendigo's attack, because it had been a willing offering. They gave themselves to it.

The wendigo had been tracking me, slowly, but surely, ever since. It had followed the same roads Veruca and I had driven on our way back to Boston. It was stopping and feeding as it went, but it was learning…the closer it got to Boston, the less evidence of its attacks it left behind. In Memphis, all they found was a partially frozen severed arm. In Pittsburgh, they never found a body at all, though the number of missing persons during the blizzard was suspiciously high.

Why so slow? Why so careful? Because it knows I'm

dangerous. It should, too. It knows it woke up because someone was walking the Shadowlands, disturbing both its sleep and the peace of the Twins. My guess was it knew that someone was me.

"*When did you figure it out?*"

"*You're not really my subconscious, are you?*"

"*Hey buddy, it's just you and me, right? What else could I be?*"

The internal dialogue was interrupted by my arrival at the rest stop. A state trooper's vehicle was parked blocking the off ramp. I pulled up beside him and waited for the trooper to come to my window.

I rolled it down as he leaned over. "Rest area is closed, sir. There's another …."

I held up the Richard Dugger employee ID. "Valente International sent me to check out the leak."

The trooper nodded, but instantly pulled back as if Valente were an infectious disease. "I'll pull out of the way, then tape off the entrance." He took another step back before asking, "Do I need to see a doctor or something? I've been out here for 45 minutes."

I put on my most scholarly face. "Usually takes at least two hours of continuous exposure, except in children or pregnant women. Still, better safe than sorry."

The officer didn't say another word as he let me in, taped up the entrance with caution tape, and sped off. That left me all alone with my car, my supplies, and my dark alter ego. Once I was sure the trooper was gone, I parked as far away from the road as possible, and gobbled down a cereal bar for both energy and good luck.

I pulled the Necronomicon from the bag, for once not fearing the strange energy that pulsed through its black leather. I flipped right to the section I was looking for, even though I had avoided it like the plague for the last three years:

"*In the dark recesses of that ancient cavern,*

I could hear the mad priest still chanting,

His deathless voice repeating the forbidden words,
Fast and frantic, an insane jumble of ranting;
Yog-Shoggoth Abishai Nostaru Nofar Immi-shoggoth.
Yog-Shoggoth Abishai Nostaru Nofar Immi-shoggoth.

Each syllable of that dark tongue echoed over water and stone and I knew then what must be done: For what horrors might come if I allowed the mad priest, the terrible mad priest to call Yog Soggoth, Walker of Shadows?"

"You ate Sarai."

"Details. Try and think big picture here, kid."

"You ate her."

17

Five feet past where Dora's bumper ended, the speckled white sidewalk gave way to raw earth. The grass was worn down by years of feet running toward the bathroom. What remained was suppressed by winter's approach. Into that cold ground, I etched a large circle with my chaos blade, then added a triangle within it, but touching at three points. At each junction, I placed an ebon candle.

Along one arm of the triangle lay the spear replica. Another arm held both my lighter and chaos blade. The base of the triangle, facing southwest, had the Necronomicon laid out upon it, open to the page I had referenced earlier. Once, it had been a spooky bedtime story for a pair of intellectuals to play with, look down upon. I tried not to think about what it meant to me now: it was both my only hope in the growing storm and the symbol of my own damnation.

After my preparations were made, I stripped down to bare skin before stepping into the center of the circle. The chill air tore into my skin, but I had a pretty hardy dose of righteous anger burning within my chest. I knelt in prayer and waited for night to come.

"Do you really think God is listening? Do you have any idea the lengths HE went to in chasing my kind out of this universe?"

Ignoring him proved easier than I thought. Just knowing that voice wasn't really a part of me made it possible.

"But I am a part of you, Colin."

The first snowflakes began to fall against the backdrop of a reddish purple sunset. I picked up the lighter and lit the candles in clockwise fashion, then tossed the lighter clear of the circle proper.

"Not to criticize, but that was our fire source. And you don't control the ground here: no exploding candle tricks."

"Nervous?"

"Curious. Even knowing you killed Sarai, suicide doesn't suit you."

"You killed Sarai, Yog Soggoth, not me. And, yes, I have a plan...but it may be better for you to kill us both now. Because once I finish this wendigo, I'm coming for you. Now that I know what you are and how you got here, I will find a way to get rid of you."

"Fair enough...but I think you may find you had a lot more say in the matter of my coming than you think."

"What's that supposed to mean?"

"Not just anyone could have called me, no matter how much virgin's blood they had on their lips."

"You're lying," I told him.

"Maybe. But how would you know? You still can't remember what happened, can you?"

"Do you want to get on with my plan or do you think you can trick me into forgiving you?"

"Give me the plan. Forgiveness is overrated."

"Take me through to the Shadowlands."

"WHAT?"

"You heard me. This thing has been living in the Shadowlands for centuries, ever since the War of the Twins. Its essence, its reality, is there. We could kill it a hundred times in the material world and it would keep coming back. I have to fight it in its world."

"And the circle is to keep our body safe from the dark energies of the realm beyond...not bad," he allowed.

"Will you take me through or do I have to do it myself?"

"Taking you is a bad idea. Getting back would be rough. But we can split the difference."

My vision of reality began to crack, as if a second world was being overlaid atop the first. A gray sea of trees crashed down upon the mud and buildings that had previously owned the scenery. The circle of dirt blazed to light with a dancing orange brilliance. The inner triangle was obscured by a dark purple mist spilling forth from the Necronomicon.

"Shadow sight...all the benefits of being there without actually having to cross over."

"But can I kill it?"

"As much as you ever could...but be careful. The Faceless trained it to be a killing machine, remember? Mad spirits taught it to eat both body and soul."

"And when did you become an expert on the Faceless?"

"When the Eye of Winter speaks, I listen. And if I am more than just your subconscious, don't you think I might know a few things about ancient cults?"

"What do you know that you're not telling me?" I wondered.

"I thought we were going our separate ways after this battle. No reason to talk about the Faceless if we're not going to work together to take them down."

"Are you why they're trying to kill me?"

"I give you shadow sight and you suddenly start getting smarter. That's why we made our pact in the first place. We can stop them, Colin. We can end the Faceless."

"But only if we stay together?"

"Like I said, you're getting smarter."

"I don't believe you."

"Tell you what. Watch how this goes down, then let me know. You want me gone, I'll leave."

18

My body was numb, though whether it was from the raging storm or from the sickening touch of the Shadowlands, I couldn't tell. If forced, I would say it was near dawn, but my sense of time was unreliable. For the longest time, I wondered if my body would still work when the wendigo showed up. Now I was starting to wonder if it would show up at all.

The passing hours allowed me to survey the surrounding terrain and my available weapons. The chaos blade was unchanged by shadow sight; it still randomly flickered across the spectrum. If I had hoped that it would seem more magical, more potent in the Shadowlands, there was nothing evidenced to reward that hope.

The faux spear of destiny had changed. Its shaft hummed with a thin red aura, the color on a Nazi armband in living Technicolor. The spear tip was lost under a coat of midnight black slime. Neither effect was overwhelming: it was indeed magical, but barely. It might have been copied from the Spear of Destiny, but its makers could only forge a spear of spite. On the other hand, steel and burning hate was not a bad option for this particular foe.

The Necronomicon's endless fount of shadow magic seemed impressive...but I remembered who was supplying my shadow sight. He may have been altering my perceptions in favor of his weapon of choice.

The world outside the circle steadily shrank as night went on. At dusk, my vision was limited only by the spectral trees blocking my line of sight. Now the blizzard around me was so intense, I could not see beyond the candlelight glow of the circle. I thought the storm was real, material, but not a single flake landed inside my circle, leaving me to wonder.

"Hey, wake up."

"Yeah, I feel it, too."

I slowly shifted my vision a little further south. At first, I thought I could see nothing but snow. Fifty feet out, though, the flakes swirled in funny patterns, painting shapes in the night air. Most were unrecognizable, but suggestively anatomical: a nose here, a tail there, a claw there. One I did recognize, and I involuntarily shuttered as I saw the face of the old curse woman, staring wickedly out at me from the storm.

I called out in that nameless, ancient tongue. "Wolf-mother, you came."

I could not pinpoint the growling voice that replied. The sound seemed to echo off every snow flake. "Step out of your circle and face me, white boy. Stop hiding and fight."

"I will fight if I must, Hungry Winter. But I would ask you to sleep, wendigo. Go back to sleep. I will return to the Shadowlands no more."

A blast of arctic wind answered me, "No sleep. It is time to eat."

My right hand crept free from my lap, ready to act if needed. The strange shapes still danced in the air, concentrated in the direction the gust had come from. No real target presented itself. "Then come, beast. I am right here. My book and I will teach you a trick the Faceless Men didn't—how to play dead like an obedient doggy."

I hoped for a quick, angry rush provoked by my words. None came and the shapes vanished from the air only to reappear twenty feet to the North. "Those you speak of will soon fill my belly, too. But they did teach us many things .... Leave your circle, Atlantean, and I will give you the death you crave."

Atlantean? I focused on the new area of icy ghosts. "Afraid of circles? That's not old knowledge. I had to teach your mate that lesson myself."

That did it. For a split second, the wendigo's rage triumphed, the snow forming a giant wolf body on the ground near the center of the swirling faces. It leapt towards me, its humongous body clearing the gap between where it was and the circle's edge effortlessly. It regained control mid-flight, but too late. With sheer will and a twitch of my hand, I forced the spear into flight, catching it in the flank. If it hadn't broken its charge, the spear would have plunged straight through its throat.

I grabbed for the chaos blade and tried to stand. My legs were used to long hours of abuse, but this night had been too much. They refused and left me eye level with its massive snout. Up close, the creature was enormous, easily six foot tall and fifteen feet long. Bright blue blood poured from its side in thick, frozen chunks.

Its breath was fetid. "Leave the circle."

I slashed out with a katana-like blade but it bobbed back just enough. It pawed at the edge, dancing around the circle, searching for an entry point, ducking whenever I brought the sword close. "You cannot hide forever, Atlantean. The cold will take you."

I shouted back, "And you'll bleed to death soon enough. That spear will kill you."

In answer, it reached back and wrenched the spear free with its teeth. A gout of its strange blood sprayed the freshly fallen snow. It looked right at me, spear in jaws, before reducing the relic to toothpicks. "A mere flesh wound, Atlantean. Leave the circle and I'll make it quick."

I swung at it again, this time willing the blade tip a foot longer in mid-swing. It bobbed back, but not enough and the lime green crystal slashed through the meat of its nose. The wound smoked and sizzled, cauterized instantly to angry scar tissue.

It roared, more in annoyance than in pain. The creature darted back into the storm, away from the circle. "Hungry Winter is not without her weapons. Die, Atlantean, die."

She turned back to charge. With each fall of her paws, the wind gathered strength. She stopped with a roar that turned into wind shear beyond anything I had ever known. My feet found it in them to stand, then kept on rising, the hurricane blast carrying me up into the air.

I crashed back down, not on my legs or my sword, but squarely on my head...and well outside my circle of protection. I'd record what happened next, but the blow was an instant knockout.

19

Wendigo, Hungry Winter, moved quickly, but cautiously around Colin's circle. The Atlantean was down, crumpled in an impossible, defenseless position. Within seconds, she was next to him. With one great paw, she rolled her meal on to its back, the better to remove the heart from the chest. His eyes began to flutter open, but it was too late. She had won.

The meal muttered to itself in a language she did not understand. It did not sound like the usual whimperings and beggings, but this meal had always been a strange one. "Mind if I have a go at it, Colin? Or do you still think you can beat it without me?"

Whatever it meant, she didn't care and plunged her teeth into its chest. Except it didn't quite happen that way. A quartet of black tendrils wrapped around her maw, slamming it shut. She reached up with her paws to claw her mouth free, but they too were quickly enveloped by a host of tentacles. One after another, the tentacles burst forth from her meal: this one coming from his palm, that one from his armpit, another five from his belly ....

Impossibly, the meal rose, standing her up, high and away from him. Wendigo struggled, but her opponent was stronger. With an effortless snap of his body, he threw her across the landscape. A trio of Shadowland trees checked her flight, but only after she'd gone straight through the trunk of one *and put dents in the other two.*

She panted. "You...you can't kill me. I am Winter, eternal. I will eat you, Atlantean."

The tentacled Atlantean paused to consider her threat. A twitch of a tentacle sent the glowing purple book flying from circle to tendril tip. "How unfortunate for you. Some fates are far worse than death." He spoke in the ancient tongue before turning his attention to the tome. The language he read from there was older still, its intonations shrill and piercing to her ears.

She charged him as he read, a frantic leap carrying her into the midst of the mighty tendrils. She would never land, her body frozen in air momentarily, before vanishing as if she'd never been there.

Yog Soggoth paused to inspect the newly inscribed artwork of a great winter wolf, before closing the Necronomicon and beginning the retreat into the depths of his host's body. "Let's see how she likes ten thousand years in the far realms beyond space and time. Maybe dog ownership will help Cthulhu's temper." Yog Soggoth smiled at that, before collapsing to the ground. He was stronger now, but his pact host was weak...and the banishing spell more difficult than it should have been. He would have to trust to luck, and his host's stubbornness, to make sure he, the Walker of Shadows, Lord of the Ancient Caverns of Insanity, Master of the Unfathomable Abyss, didn't die of hypothermia.

EPILOGUE

was still walking with a limp when Valente's Christmas party rolled around. The party was Inner Circle only. That meant two things: One, everybody thought they were a big shot; two, the cost of the buffet and bar could have fed all the starving kids in Africa for the next decade.

I wanted to think I was the exception to the inflated ego norm of the room. I wasn't. I was on the arm of a beautiful woman considered dangerous even by the standards of these lunatics. My inability to discuss how I lost the top of my left ear to frostbite or where I picked up my limp made me mysterious. In absence of facts, rumors flowed. My favorite held that I had called forth an ice demon to snow under Wall Street for 48 hours, allowing Valente to avoid what otherwise might have been disastrous financial losses. I wasn't about to correct them and not just because I wasn't sure what had happened that night myself. In a room full of assassins, telepaths, and corporate espionage experts, professional demon summoner was a reputation to be envied.

Veruca and I were doing all right, though I'd hurt her feelings by not inviting her along for the wendigo hunt. I had told her most of what had happened, but I thought she thought I was holding out on her. Nobody likes a story with an unknown ending. We still got along well, with her spending most of her off hours in my apartment, but it felt like there was a distance growing between us.

I could have closed the gap, but I didn't. I knew what Veruca was and accepted her as she was. She didn't know what I was. Making a pact was one thing…but I knew now how woefully inadequate that description was for me. Yog Soggoth, an ancient evil from beyond the limits of reality, lived inside of me. I didn't make a deal with the devil. I was the devil.

The night of the storm changed that relationship, too. For my part, I had finally come to grips with what I was: part-Harvard dropout, part Old One. For its part, Yog Soggoth understood his limitations. He needed me, though I'm not sure either of us understood why. It was like he had one tentacle in me and another still firmly anchored in his prison beyond the walls of the universe. Without me and my body, he might as well still be trapped there.

Something had changed regarding Sarai that night, too. I had poured through countless deceased Jane Doe reports, tales of women with amnesia, and other reports Valente had sent my way. But in my time in the Shadowlands, the time when Yog Soggoth and I were one, I felt…something. Sarai was alive, even if only in my dreams. Yog Soggoth had done something with her, hidden her somewhere, maybe even tucked her away in whatever prison Yog Soggoth had rotted in since the creation of the world. I still didn't know what had happened to her, but I did know there was a chance to get her back.

THE END

Thank you for reading! Find book two of the Modern Knights novels coming in 2017.

Please sign up for the City Owl Press newsletter for chances to win special subscriber-only contests and giveaways as well as receiving information on upcoming releases and special excerpts.

Joshua Bader

www.facebook.com/joshua.bader.50

All reviews are welcome and appreciated. Please consider leaving one on your favorite social media and book buying sites.

For books in the world of romance and speculative fiction that embody Innovation, Creativity, and Affordability, check out City Owl Press at www.cityowlpress.com.

ACKNOWLEDGEMENTS

The following acknowledgements will most certainly miss multiple people of great importance... You have my sincerest apologies for the oversight and my deepest gratitude for your contributions.

I want to thank my wife and daughters for their patience and tolerating those times when I disappear into the solitude of my writing. They are both my reason for publishing and my surest ground when I need to return to reality. Josiah, you missed out on this book (aside from a few kicks from inside a pregnant belly), but I assure you, you'll have your chance to get in on future acknowledgements.

I want to thank both Yelena Casale and Tina Moss for their help in editing the book and their belief in my voice. I hope this is the beginning of great things for all of us. I would be remiss not to include all the City Owl Press authors and the group Facebook discussion for their encouragement and inspiration.

I certainly did not invent the genre of urban fantasy. While I first met it in the works of C.S. Lewis, I owe a deep debt to Stephen King, Dean Koontz, Jim Butcher, and Laurell Hamilton for developing both the genre and my imagination. If my characters are half as real to the reader as Harry Dresden or Anita Blake are to me, then I am honored.

I owe a debt to those groups of gamers who let me practice and develop my storytelling voice and the individual names would overwhelm the size of this page. Whether it was in my home, yours, or at one of our live action settings, I thank you for the opportunity and hope you all had as much fun as I did. Tim and Joe, I owe special thanks to both of you.

A special thanks to Norman Public Schools for giving me the time that I needed to finish this project.

ABOUT THE AUTHOR

J oshua Bader is a retired professional vagabond wizard who now leads a much more settled life in Oklahoma City. He dabbles in the mystic arts of writing, mathematics education, pizza delivery, and parenting. He shares his sacred space with his wife, two daughters, three dogs, and a cat, with a baby boy adding to the chaos in April 2016. Josh holds a masters in psychology from OU, but his wizarding license has been temporarily suspended due to a suspicious frogging incident.

ABOUT THE PUBLISHER

City Owl Press is a cutting edge indie publishing company, bringing the world of romance and speculative fiction to discerning readers.

www.cityowlpress.com

CPSIA information can be obtained at www.ICGtesting.com
Printed in the USA
LVOW11s1450170616

493059LV00001B/96/P